In Their Shoes

Sandip Khade

Published By

Redgrab Books Pvt. Ltd.

942, Mutthiganj, Prayagraj, 211003

www.redgrabbooks.com

contact@redgrabbooks.com

Price in india : 200/- INR

First published by Redgrab Books in 2022

Copyright © 2022 Redgrab Books Pvt. Ltd.

Copyright Text © 2022 Sandip Khade

Printed and bound in India

Cover Design & Typesetting by Redgrab Books team

ISBN : 978-93-90944-04-0

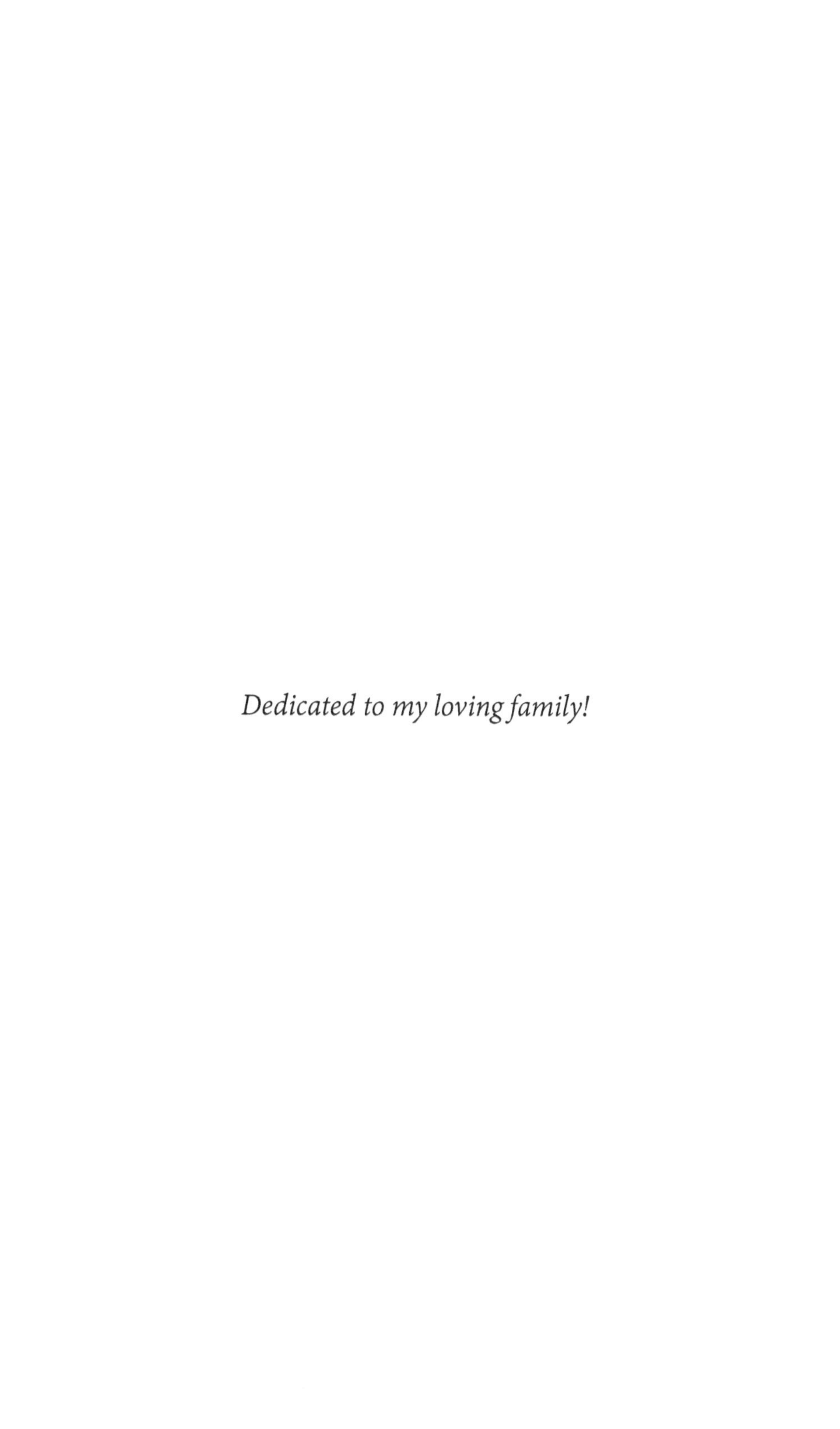

Dedicated to my loving family!

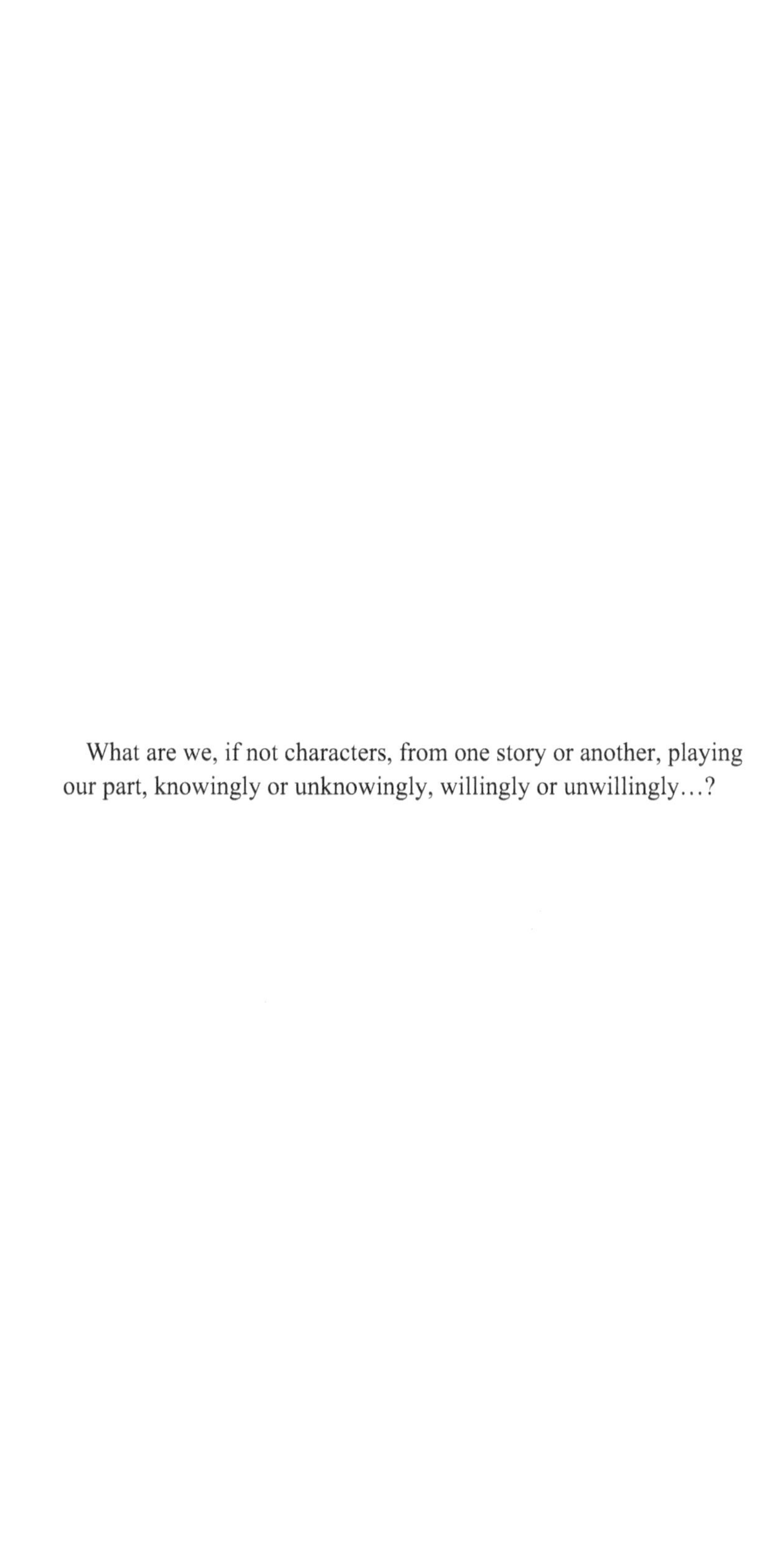

What are we, if not characters, from one story or another, playing our part, knowingly or unknowingly, willingly or unwillingly…?

About Author

Sandip Khade was born and raised in Mumbai. He holds bachelor's degree in Information Technology and works with an IT firm. When not working, he likes to travel, explore places, and write. Sandip has keen interest in the Mystery genre, and *In Their Shoes* is his second Novel.

Sandip can be reached at sandpkhade@gmail.com

Acknowledgment

I am hugely indebted to my Editor, Varsha Naik, without whom this book would not have been possible. I am grateful to Rukhsar Sayed and Nishtha Singh for giving their invaluable comments; and to Sana Shaikh, Hayley Davis, and Tejas Bhagat for not. I want to thank Mohini Deshwali for cleaning up the mess and making this book more readable. Most importantly, I want to thank the reader for showing interest and picking up this book; I hope you find this worth your time.

CONTENTS

PROLOGUE

It was a small room, illuminated by golden orange light emanating from two big square diffuser lights kept on either side of a black leather couch; the one Arnav was sharing with Mithila - a renowned author. At a few feet of distance, Radhika, editor of a prominent media house, was sitting on an old-fashioned wooden chair, engaged in conversation with Mithila.

The walls were painted in a cream colour and speckled with brown. There were few stools kept upside down in the corners, and antique frames were placed on them, propped against the wall. On the right side of the couch, the wall was lined with a rack with books of various genres. Arnav found the setting rather odd as he read out the titles of the books to himself. The fact that the names of these novels and their authors were alien to him made Arnav feel uneasy. Though the air conditioning system in the room was on, Arnav felt a drop of sweat trickling down the back of his neck.

A week earlier, when Arnav had received a call from his manager regarding this meeting, Arnav wanted to say no, but somehow he had ended up saying yes as it was required for "marketing" purposes. And now, as he sat in the room with Mithila to his left, composed and calm, sipping her coffee and answering questions as though it was her daily job, Arnav found himself wondering if coming here for an interview was a good idea.

"You must be a voracious reader too," Radhika asked Arnav, expecting a jaw-dropping number in reply, maybe higher than what Mithila had just shared.

Arnav didn't reply; her words never reached him. He was still not able to digest the fact that this all was real – that he was an author and was sitting next to the woman because of whom he had started writing – and not just a page from a story someone was reading. I mean, what were the odds of that happening. But still, it would have been way simpler that way, Arnav thought to himself.

"Oh, is it that big number?" Radhika interrupted Arnav's thoughts.

"No," Arnav answered at once. "To tell you the truth, I don't like reading." A trace of nervousness accompanied his words, "And I have just crossed two digits."

Arnav smiled, leaned forward, picked up the cup from the table, and took a few sips of coffee. Radhika looked at him curiously, a quizzical expression plastered on her face. Arnav had expected this; Long back, when he was one book old, someone had told him that to be a writer, you need to be a reader first.

"That's interesting. If not reading, what inspired you to become a writer?" Radhika appeared sceptical as she continued.

"It's a long story and probably boring too." Arnav offered as he kept the cup back on the table, trying hard to dodge the question.

I should not have come here, Arnav muttered to himself. *This was a bad idea.*

"No offense," Mithila interjected. "but I think that's not the author's or storyteller's job to decide. That part should be left for the audience."

"Fine," Arnav sighed, giving in, "don't say I didn't warn you in the beginning."

Arnav was mum for some time as he collected pieces from his memories before he started.

"It all began when I was an engineering student. It was my last semester, and I was in the library reading a newspaper. I still had half an hour before my exam. There was an article titled – *Beauty with Brain.* The picture next to the article showed a girl wearing an orange top and blue jeans."

Arnav paused and looked down at his fingers.

"I thought she was a model," Arnav said and smiled despite himself, "but apparently, she was an editor in a publication house."

Arnav found himself being pulled back into the memories.

"I don't know what it was, her face, the ink-dark tousled hair which fell over her shoulder in ringlets, or her month-old-baby-like eyes which did the trick. Maybe it was her eyes; They always do the trick. I felt something I had never felt before." Arnav paused again to check if they were still interested in the story or if he should stop. He found Radhika and Mithila's eyes riveted on him, all ears.

"And I don't know how high I was, but I thought if I could write something, and get it published through the publishing house she was working in, I would get a chance to meet her." Arnav paused when he perceived how idiotic that might have sounded.

"So, you are telling us that you started writing because you wanted to meet someone?" Radhika questioned, completely flabbergasted.

Arnav didn't say anything but just nodded.

"I sat straight through days and nights for weeks until I had written something we could call as a first draft of a book." Arnav continued.

"And how many books had you read before trying your hand at writing?" Radhika glanced at Mithila for a few seconds before she looked back at Arnav and queried. She thought Arnav was trying to pull some prank on her.

Arnav hesitated for a moment before he answered, "Well, apart from educational ones, zero."

"You have got to be kidding me!"

Again, Arnav nodded and smiled, feeling more embarrassed with each passing second, and thinking he should not be here.

"Writing is a lot like falling in love." The words were now coming in whispers as if he was speaking to himself. "Those who have experienced it know that it just happens, and you have to move with the flow; you cannot plan it. But getting published is like making another person fall in love with you. And trust me, it's a heck of a job when they have better options than you." Arnav said and took another sip of coffee.

"That's interesting!" Radhika opened the book she was holding in her hand and turned a few pages.

May I?

The words crawled in Arnav's ears, knocked on his brain's wall and begged for his attention.

In a blink of an eye, the scene around him changed. Arnav screwed his eyes as he adjusted them to a dimly lit room. He was still sitting, not on a couch, but on a wooden chair that groaned as he shifted in it. The lamp perched on the table in front of him glowed golden orange, dimly illuminating the dusty, old alehouse he was in.

It was almost past midnight, Arnav deduced by the number of people who were sitting around other tables and the yawn he tried to stifle. It appeared to be a small room, or maybe it was the gloom that was doing the trick.

What was that? Arnav questioned himself as he recalled the conversation he had just dreamed of having with someone before he looked at the papers scattered on the table in front of him.

'May I?' The Man who was standing next to Arnav's table, whom Arnav hadn't noticed until now, said again. He pulled up an empty chair and sat across the table without waiting for Arnav's reply. Arnav straightened up in his chair as he recognized the face.

"Working on a new novel." The man remarked as his eyes strayed to the scattered papers.

"Why are you here?" Arnav asked, ignoring the man's comment.

"I had one question; I thought I would come and ask you." The man answered.

Arnav looked at him blankly, trying to figure out where this conversation was going.

"What would happen if someday someone finds out about you, about what you have done? What if that mask falls from your face and someone sees the monster that lies behind?" The man continued as he tore his gaze from the papers in front of him and looked straight into Arnav's eyes.

"I don't understand," Arnav said.

The man rummaged in his jacket and produced a piece of paper from his pocket. "I am here to tell you how it will end."

"What is this?" Arnav looked at the piece of paper the man was holding.

The man slid the paper across the table towards Arnav. "It's an Alibi – well, not literally. But you will find out soon enough what it means."

Arnav perused through the paper, oblivious to the fact that the man slowly pushed back his chair, got to his feet, and walked out of the alehouse.

Arnav sighed, slumped lower in his chair, and sat there for some time, staring blankly at the flickering lamp before he gathered his things and thoughts, realizing it was about time.

Arnav crossed the road and continued walking on the paved path. Above him, the sky was a mass of dark black clouds and appeared ominous; at a distance, a lightning bolt divided it into two, and rain started pouring down in sheets. Arnav sped up as his house hove into view, and yet he was completely drenched by the time he reached there.

The wooden gate of the compound creaked when he opened it, as if complaining about waking it from a deep sleep. Arnav entered and closed the gate behind him. The house in front of him appeared empty as he covered the distance towards it. Doors and windows were closed; the lights were off.

"Has she gone to bed?" Arnav wondered as he pulled the hood back from his head and ruffled his hair.

Arnav glanced around his neighbourhood as he pressed the bell and waited; The world had gone to sleep. When minutes passed and nothing happened, he pressed the bell again. He checked his watch as he waited impatiently; Night had already turned a few hours older.

Arnav eventually gave up and considered the possibility of her going to sleep. He fetched his phone and dialled her number. He shoved one hand in his pocket as the other held the phone near his ear. The night was surprisingly cold, and his hands were already shaking.

Though it wasn't evident on his face, he panicked when she didn't answer the call. He stared at the screen of his phone for a moment and hit the dial again. It was strange. It had never happened that she had gone to sleep before he returned home. It didn't matter how late it was, midnight or early morning; she was always awake. Sometimes simply waiting for him to return home, sometimes lost in her work. *But then there is always a first time*, Arnav told himself as she didn't answer the second call either.

Arnav put his phone back in his pocket and stood there, resting his head against the door. He found himself dwelling on the memory of the last time he had reached home early in the morning.

"You haven't gone to sleep yet." Arnav had remarked as she opened the door within a few seconds of him pressing the bell as if she

was standing on the other side of the door waiting for him.

"I still have some work I need to finish." She had responded, avoiding eye contact as she closed the door and followed him into the hall. She always did that when she lied, he knew.

"Really?" Arnav slouched down on the couch, searching for the files and documents usually scattered on the table next to the couch. The files were closed, and the documents were kept in a pile. He didn't say anything further and waited for her to meet his eyes.

"Okay, you got me." She gave in when their eyes met, and then sank onto the couch next to him. Her hand moved through his hair before she planted a kiss on his cheek.

Arnav had then wrapped his hand around her as she rested her head on his chest and kissed her head.

"I cannot sleep without knowing you are home." She had confided in him then.

"I know." Arnav had said and smiled, thinking how lucky he was to have someone like her in his life.

"And you are getting thinner with each passing day too." There was a long silence before she spoke again, making him think that she had fallen asleep.

"So, I want to ensure you are not skipping dinner." She carried on as she looked up into his eyes and then hauled herself to her feet.

"But I never skip dinner." Arnav had argued as he grabbed her hand in time and stopped her from heading towards the kitchen, "even if I have it for breakfast."

"Really?" She had smiled coyly as she tried to free her hand.

"Really." Arnav had responded before pulling her onto himself.

Arnav had then laid back on the couch, his arms straining her and not allowing her to go. She simply gave in and got lost in his eyes. He tucked the stray hairs behind her ears and pecked her nose before moving down to her lips.

"If you don't want me to be awake and open the door for you when you return home," she had said as they broke the kiss, her hand still running through his hair, "why do you ring the bell despite having a

     In Their Shoes

"Idiot!" Arnav murmured as he snapped back from his reverie. His hand rummaged through his pocket and found the key there. The door was now cold against his forehead. He pulled the key out as he stepped back, plunged it in the lock, and pushed through the door. He entered quietly, gingerly kept the key in the bowl on the shoe rack and closed the door behind him. His eyes stayed on the shelf for a few seconds as they searched for a note he thought she might have kept for him, but there wasn't one. He wriggled out of his jacket, hung it on a door hook, and blundered towards the hall.

Arnav paused in his tracks as he saw a silhouette of a person. She was awake, sitting on the couch, propped against a cushion, lost in her thoughts. In front of her, on the table, a candle flickered as it tried to fight with darkness, but eventually guttered out. The song playing on the music player muffled the sound of the rain which was falling outside in sheets. The flare of the lighter lit his face, and a new candle flickered to life, standing next to the stubs of other candles.

"You are still awake," Arnav said as he kept the lighter back on the table. She didn't reply or move. Her eyes were still staring blankly at the photo that hugged the wall opposite to the couch; it was slightly askew, as if someone had tried removing it but then gave up. Arnav couldn't gauge her mood as he stood there. He had never seen her like this before. With thoughts about what might have happened running in the back of his mind, he walked towards the wall to adjust the photo.

"How do you feel when you kill someone?" Arnav had hardly taken a few steps when her question stopped him. "I mean in your books."

Arnav froze, and it was then that he noticed the floor was littered with papers; the ones he had hoped wouldn't fall into her hands.

"Do you feel guilty? Or you tell yourself that you did what was needed to be done?" She added; her voice was strangely close now.

Arnav was still staring at the papers. A part of him told him that it was not what he thought it was, but then deep inside, he knew it was lying. There was no other explanation for her behaviour, and he desperately hoped he was wrong.

She was standing right in front of him when he turned around. His eyes strayed to her bare legs before falling on her face. Her sea-blue eyes, deep yet still, were searching his. She was trying to find someone in them he knew wasn't there.

"There are times," Arnav whispered as he reached for her hand and caressed it gently before holding it, "when you are left with no other options. It becomes necessary..."

"For what?" She mumbled, her voice barely a whisper.

Arnav moved closer as he covered the space that was separating them. They were so close that they could feel the warmth of each other's breath. There were lots of things that he wanted to tell her, but then he wasn't sure if she would understand.

"You are a monster," a disembodied voice hissed near Arnav's ear.

"Closure." Arnav simply answered as he wrapped his left hand around her waist and planted a kiss on her lips.

A few heartbeats later, a bullet shell bounced on the floor, filling the air with an acrid smell. Blood gushed out of the wound where the bullet had kissed skin and ran down in rivulets from the shirt, leaving its trace behind. Arnav released her and watched her stagger back before she flopped down on the couch.

"Why?" She asked, deeply hurt.

"When this is all over, I want you to remember me," Arnav said, ignoring her question, "not as a night that I am, but someone who met the beautiful morning that you are."

And then, another shot rang out.

1 – Parul Kasbekar

"I have seen it happen many times, even when the people sitting in this room, including lawyers, investigating officers, judge, and the ones who are not in the room but are following the trials, know that the guy standing here in this box is a culprit, or in some cases is not and is being wrongly framed, but the court is forced to give a verdict that is not accurate due to lack of the evidence. But not today." Parul was finding it hard to breathe as she spoke, her face damp with sweat. She wiped it with back of her hand before continuing. Though her voice wasn't loud enough, there was pin-drop silence in the courtroom, and everyone listened to her with rapt attention.

"Here, these are the things I have found out since the first trial of this case." She handed over the documents, "It has the evidence which will shed light on the facts that have been missed in the investigation or purposely been kept hidden from the investigating officers."

The judge scrutinized the girl standing before him, telling him that the facts and evidence presented in front of him were wrong, and the man who he was going to set free was not innocent. It was a bold claim, which he couldn't deny without considering the documents she had brought forth. He wore his black-rimmed spectacles and perused the documents he was holding in his hands.

Parul heaved a sigh and waited as the judge studied the documents. She was glad she had made it to the court in time before the judge could deliver the verdict and set one more culprit free to roam the streets.

There were a few minutes of silence in the court before the judge spoke.

"I think these should be enough to charge him." He tore his eyes from the documents and looked at Parul, "Thank you for your effort; the court appreciates it."

Parul stood there without saying anything, thinking she had finally done it.

"Looking at the new evidence and facts Ms. Parul has brought in front of the court..."

Parul's cell phone beeped, and her eyes shot open to the view of the ceiling with peeling plaster. That's how she woke up, always. Her hand involuntarily travelled to her right and turned off the alarm. She then lay awake on her bed, staring blankly at the ceiling fan which looked tired and aged, and dwelled on the fact that life had thrown another day at her to survive.

Sometimes Parul felt like not getting up from the bed, skipping her job and all other activities. But then she had bills to pay and a life to live. Parul hated this, her life, and not knowing where it was going. It sucked, waking up every morning, getting ready, and then walking into that office, where nobody cared about her; half of the office didn't know she worked there, and the remaining half didn't understand why she worked there.

Almost a year back, when Parul had given the interview and got the job, she was happy, realising she was finally going to do what she had wanted to do since she was a kid; And mainly, she was going to Mumbai – the dream city. But then, as the months passed, she discovered everything was different from what she had imagined; but then, after all, it was her imagination, it wasn't the city or people's fault.

Parul had thought she would cover stories, dig up information, and reveal the truth to put criminals behind bars or pull innocents out of jail. But what she was doing – making coffee or tea, taking printouts, and delivering it to their owner; and sometimes, when the person whom she reported to was happy or excited about something he had found, he would allow her to read his findings and tell her how cool it was.

Parul would feel sick and full of despair, and though she didn't show it, she felt jealous of them. She yearned for the life she saw them living. *One day,* Parul would murmur when she was full of despair, *I will get there. But when?* She had asked herself this question a zillion times but was yet to find the answer.

There were days Parul would feel like resigning from her job and moving back to her hometown. But then what would she do or tell her parents? And what about the relatives and the people there; they would get something juicy to talk about. Parul would quickly push away the thought along with the snatches of conversation she would hear people talking about a girl living alone in a city and then suddenly returning home leaving her job without any explanation.

 In Their Shoes

Parul knew her parents would somehow understand; but then she also knew they would ask her the question she had always dodged. *When will you get married?*

Parul was fed up answering it again and again. She couldn't understand why they didn't accept that even though she was a girl, she had the rights to decide with whom she wanted to spend her life; and she hadn't found the right person yet.

Parul sighed as she sat up, arching her hands above her head before tying her ink-dark hairs into a knot, leaving a few stranded hairs to fall on her forehead. As she scanned the small bedroom that was cramped with a study table, one small cupboard, and her bed, she found someone sleeping next to her, his half-naked body wrapped in a blanket and head hidden under the pillow. As she stared at him, she had a sinking feeling that told her that even this wasn't going to last long like her previous relationships. She wasn't even sure if she would get to see him again. To be frank, she couldn't even recall his face or anything about him; the only thing she remembered was that he was good in bed, a bit aggressive and wild. The reason she still felt tired. But then, she couldn't deny that was how she liked it.

Parul had dated a handful of guys, but none of the relationships had lasted longer than a few months, some only a few weeks, and some lasted only for a night, which she later discovered was what they called one-night stands. She ultimately stopped seeing guys and promised she wouldn't do this to herself after the previous guy she dated stopped taking her calls after spending two nights at her house. But last night, when she saw *him,* there was something about him that made her head over and start the conversation. It was usually the other way around.

After a few drinks, they headed to her place, and the next thing she knew, they were in her bedroom, and he was pulling off her clothes. And then they made love, or that's what she always told herself when she spent the night with someone.

Parul walked into the bathroom to brush her teeth, and then splashed some water on her face. She traced a path towards the kitchen, recalling that she hadn't eaten anything last night. She grumbled as she opened the fridge and found only two slices of bread left in the packet, and the bottle of the jam was empty. She settled down at the table with a glass of milk and the bread.

"Great!" Parul muttered under her breath as she found the handwritten note on the fridge reminding her that she hadn't paid the rent yet.

Parul walked back into the bedroom and felt like waking him up and kicking his ass out of the house before he could ditch her; But then the next moment thought of taking a chance and didn't wake him. She wrote a note saying she was going out for a walk and put her cell number at the end. She then slipped into her track pants and walked out of her apartment, closing the door behind her.

Parul wanted to go for a walk, but as she descended the staircase, she decided to take the cycle out. She plugged her earphones in her ears, put the phone in her pocket, pulled on her hoodie, and started pedalling.

Parul had covered some distance and was dwelling on her thoughts when her cycle stopped with a jerk. Her heart was almost in her throat when she snapped back to attention.

"Shit, Shit!" Parul muttered as she saw she had bumped into a car, which resembled an Audi R8. Parul quickly got down and walked towards the driver's door, cursing under her breath. Though her cycle hadn't caused significant damage to the car, she knew that even a tiny dent would mean a month's salary. And she couldn't afford it.

Parul stopped in her tracks as she saw the driver's head perched on the steering wheel, blood dripping from his hair. The windshield was broken. She then registered that the Audi had bumped into another car, a Swift. That car had suffered more damage than the Audi, and so had the girls in it. One of the girl's head was on the steering wheel and covered with shattered glass; the other girl's upper body was hanging out of the opened door.

Parul's heartbeat increased as she walked towards them. Her hand was shaking when she checked the girl's breathing. She staggered back as she discerned that the girl was dead. She pulled out her phone and dialled some numbers as she struggled to breathe.

2 - Soham Deshmukh

Does one know when they are dead? Do they feel anything at all? Or does life just end, and then nothing happens?

These questions thronged in Soham's mind as he drifted back into consciousness; he was going to discover the truth soon.

Soham felt strangely light, as if he was floating in the air. He wasn't sure where he was, but the place was strangely quiet. As if someone had turned off the volume in his ears, or maybe he turned deaf. The surrounding darkness made him blind, making him feel like he was losing his senses one after another.

Soham didn't consider himself a religious man, nor did he ever believe in God. Still, from the snatches of conversation he had heard from two old drunk men not long ago, if he was dead, he was indeed in one room waiting for his turn to be produced in front of whoever was to decide his fate; whether he should be sent to heaven or hell.

Soham wasn't interested in their talk on that day as he had walked in, and anyway, it wasn't them but the liquor that was doing the talking. He, however, didn't have any other option but to sit next to them. He didn't believe this though, at least not then; but now? He wasn't sure. Now he felt as if that talk was some sort of indication for him about where his life was heading.

Soham closed his eyes and waited.

Hell!

Soham heard a voice, which he knew had come from somewhere deep within him. A few minutes passed before Soham felt a gentle touch on his shoulder. *It's time;* he told himself and took a deep breath, preparing himself to face whatever was coming. Soham tried to move but registered that he was tied to the spot with something. He then tried moving his right hand, and suddenly a searing pain shot up from his fingers to his head. The pain was so severe he cursed himself for trying to move his hand. He felt like cutting off his hand and ending it. Soham then tried moving his other hand; a pang of panic shot up his body when he didn't feel it, as if it wasn't there. Before he could fathom what was happening, he was unconscious again.

People say that when you are dying, your whole life flashes in front of you. Maybe it's true, or Soham was just recalling the incidents of last night.

Soham found himself perched on the edge of a wooden stool, his hands resting on either side of the glass he had just emptied. He was trying to wash down his feelings with liquor; it hadn't helped so far.

The world around him spun, focusing in and out as if someone was adjusting a microscope. He stared at the glass in front of him as a waiter refilled it. He had enough drinks, he knew, but lately that was the only way he knew to handle his life. He stared at the glass for a few seconds, watching the tiny droplets race down its length as he contemplated how it all had come to this. When he failed to find answers, he simply raised his glass and emptied it. He kept the glass back on the table and would have asked the waiter to refill it, had not his head flopped down next to the empty glass.

It was some time before Soham regained consciousness. This time, however, when he tried opening his eyes, the room wasn't dark. As his eyes adjusted to the surroundings, he realised he was sitting in a car and not in any room, his face resting on the steering wheel. He felt a metallic taste in his mouth, and it didn't take him long to perceive it was his blood.

Soham's body screamed with pain for every slight movement he tried to make. When he felt exhausted and spent, he gave up and sat like that, his breathing ragged and laborious. His head felt heavy, and he perceived that his hair was wet, as if he had just taken a shower. He closed his eyes and waited, recalling if he had.

"Where were you last night? You didn't even return my calls." Soham asked her when she had finally answered.

Soham was again walking down the memory lane, recalling bits and pieces.

"We were out, celebrating the new project we got, I had told you. And I had forgotten my cell in the car." She had responded. There was something in her voice that didn't sound right.

Soham wanted to say something but stopped himself. He didn't want to start an argument again. This was just a bad phase in their relationship, he knew. He just didn't know how to handle it.

In Their Shoes

Soham had met her at his sister Asmita's engagement ceremony and had fallen for her at first sight. He had approached her after the engagement, and they exchanged numbers after a small talk. Within weeks he found himself talking with her on the phone for hours about random things. And before they knew it, they were both madly in love. After dating for a few months, they both decided to announce their relationship to their families, but then life happened, and things started falling apart. It wasn't their fault; it was just the circumstances surrounding them which were playing their part.

"Hey, listen." She continued when he didn't say anything. "I have to go; I haven't taken a shower yet."

"Okay, we will talk later." Soham had said reluctantly when all he wanted was to tell her how much he missed her.

"Sure, bye." She had replied, oblivious of his feelings.

"Bye, take care." Soham returned, but the line was already dead.

Soham opened his eyes and tried to lift his head one more time and felt he needed to call someone for help. Soham bit his tongue and winced in pain as he rested his head on the headrest. The windshield in front of him was shattered, obstructing the view of what was on the other side of it. The steering wheel and the airbag on which his head was resting a few seconds back had turned red. He couldn't tell what colour it had before.

Soham felt dizzy when he discovered blood was streaming down his face; He gathered that the pain he felt on the back of his head was probably from pieces of glass. He sat there, leaning his back against the seat, motionless, wishing it was a bad dream. He closed his eyes and waited as time crawled by at tortoise speed.

This moment was the first time when Soham thought about the pain his parents must have endured, for they had died in an accident a few months back. They were returning from an event at night when their car had plunged into a ditch. By the time someone found them, it was the next morning, and it was late by then. They had suffered severe injuries and blood loss and were declared dead on reaching the hospital. Soham wondered if he was destined to die the same way. If he indeed was, there were things he wanted to do, people he wanted to see for the last time.

Soham thought of his sister then and what she would do when she discovered that her brother had suffered the same fate as her parents. She had somehow recovered from their parent's loss, or that's what she pretended; but would she from his? He asked himself. He slowly drifted towards unconsciousness as he tried to find the answer.

"Where are you going now?" Asmita had asked as Soham pushed away the plate and stood up. He didn't feel like eating, nor did he have answers to her questions. To be frank, he didn't have answers to the questions which thronged his mind either.

"I need a drink." Soham had retorted as he walked away from the table and closed the door behind him.

Voices from his surroundings pulled Soham back to reality. From the corner of his eye, he saw people surrounding his car. He tried to understand what they were saying, but none of them made any sense. On his right, he saw one guy moving others away as he put something in the gap between the window glass and door. There was an unusual sound, and the next second the guy pulled open the door.

"This is going to hurt." He said as he leaned forward and gingerly unlatched the seat belt, the thing Soham had thought of doing but had given up, fearing the pain he couldn't bear.

As the guy removed the belt, pain shot up Soham's body again, making him wish he was dead instead. He wanted to scream but bit his tongue and let them pull him out of the car. The moment he was out and tried to bear his weight on his legs, the world whirled around him, and he flopped down on the ground.

"Sir!"

Soham heard a disembodied voice. He tried to open his eyes so he could locate the source. As Soham lifted his face and looked at his surroundings, he deduced that he was in that pub again.

"We are closing."

Soham got up and paid the bill before staggering towards the exit. He did everything to not fall to the ground, for he knew he didn't have enough strength to pull himself to his feet again. Once he was in the parking lot, he walked towards his car and struggled with his keys before he finally opened the door and turned the ignition on.

                                    In Their Shoes

Soham changed the gear and pressed the accelerator harder once he was on an empty road. He was trying hard to keep his eyes open and on the road. He drove for a few minutes before a car hove into view. He didn't slow down but instead blew the horn; the car however didn't allow him to pass. Soham panicked as he saw the distance closing between him and the car that was ahead of him. When he saw they were going to collide, he pressed hard at the break, hoping he had enough time to pull the car to a halt. His car, however, accelerated, and before Soham registered his mistake, he had rammed his car into the one in front of him.

The driver in the other car lost control and rammed into the divider. It all happened fast, and before Soham could blink, he had lost consciousness.

"Hello."

Soham heard the voice again. This time it wasn't the waiter.

"Can you hear me?"

The guy who had pulled Soham out of his car stooped next to him, put Soham's arm around his neck, and hauled him to his feet. Soham was slowly drifting back to consciousness. He didn't say anything but simply blinked.

Soham heard the ambulance siren, and in no time there were two men standing beside him with a stretcher. Soham refused and instead preferred walking toward the ambulance with whatever strength he had left in him.

Soham saw a few more men with stretchers in their hands walk past him when the gravity of the situation struck him. He stopped dead in his tracks and tried to turn around, fearing the worst. Soham felt his heart slowing down as he saw them pulling out the first girl before they put her body on the stretcher and covered her with the white cloth. Soham froze as he saw them pull the body of the second girl out. When the reality that both the girls were dead hit him, he crumpled down on the ground, wishing one more time that he was dead.

3 - Arnav Inamdar

Arnav tossed and turned in his sleep and found himself drifting back to his childhood memories. He was back in the room, sitting in a corner, his knees close to his chest, his arms wrapped around them. He buried his face in the gap between his knees and chest, wishing he would disappear somehow. His body was shaking as he begged the disembodied voices to go away. He couldn't see them, for the room was engulfed in darkness.

"Just go away," Arnav screamed, his voice lost in his throat.

Arnav was just twelve years old and wasn't sure what was wrong with him or what was happening. Arnav dreamt of two kids sitting by a lake, which was followed by one of them drowning in that lake. And then Arnav would find himself in the shoes of another kid as some older man pulled him away from the crowd which had thronged near the lake and hiss in his ears – you are a monster; you don't deserve to live.

Arnav sat in the corner like a crumpled piece of paper and waited. Suddenly there was pin-drop silence, and the storeroom grew cold. He felt as though the volume in his ears had been turned down.

"YOU are a monster," a disembodied voice hissed near his ear again when he had gathered some courage and was going to look up.

"No, I am not!" Arnav shot back, and the next moment light crept into the room as someone opened the door.

Arnav screwed his eyes as he adjusted them to the light and saw his mom running towards him, followed by his dad.

"What happened?" She pulled him closer and embraced him.

Arnav's dad stood there without saying a word. Look on his face told Arnav that this wasn't the first time they had found him this way. There was something in his dad's eyes that told Arnav that he agreed with the voices Arnav heard. Arnav's mom then walked him back to his room while his dad trailed them; he was speaking on the phone with someone, telling them that it was time.

"You need some sleep." Arnav's mom said once they were in his room.

Arnav nodded without saying anything and climbed on the bed. His mom then kissed his forehead as her hand ruffled his hair. She was worried; Arnav could tell by the way she looked at him. It was the reason he couldn't understand. She then turned off the lamp and left the room.

"I told you we need to shift him there; they have all the provisions for handling such cases." Arnav heard his dad talking on the other side of the door. They were standing outside the room and speaking in hushed voices. Arnav pressed his ear close to the door and tried to listen to what they were discussing.

"He is not a case," Arnav heard his mom snapping back at his dad. "He is our son." Her voice was barely a whisper when she added this. She was crying. Arnav wanted to open the door and see what was happening but found it locked from the outside.

"I know," Arnav's dad retorted. "You think I don't care about him?"

There was silence on the other side of the door, and Arnav could hear his mom sniffing now.

"We don't have any option." His dad repeated.

"We have one..." Arnav's mom objected.

"She couldn't help then; she cannot help now," his dad reminded her, marking the end of the conversation.

Arnav woke up with a debilitating headache, something he was used to – a hangover. He pressed the pillow harder with his hand as he buried his head under it. He was lying in bed on his stomach, every inch of his body screaming with pain as if complaining about the things he had done last night.

Arnav closed his eyes and wished the pain would go away, but it didn't. It never did. He had heard the alarm, but it went off within a second before he could get up and turn it off himself. He wondered if there was an alarm, or it was just his imagination; He wasn't sure. He didn't care as long as that sound didn't buzz again.

Arnav heard the humming sound of a ceiling fan and wished it to stop. *I need to take care of that thing,* he cursed under his breath as he pressed the pillow harder, trying to smother the pain. Then he recalled he didn't have a ceiling fan in his bedroom; he turned around in bed, lying on his back, and threw the pillow away to stare at the ceiling above. There was indeed a fan, which appeared as if it would fall at any time.

Arnav sat upright and looked around the bedroom. It wasn't his; he was in someone else's residence. But then again, he was used to that. What he wasn't used to was the empty space next to him on the bed; a girl was always there, her naked body wrapped in a bed sheet. But surprisingly, there wasn't anyone there now.

Arnav closed his eyes and tried to recall if he had indeed hooked up with someone last night. He had. There was no other explanation for waking up in someone else's home. But then, where was she now? Had they checked into some hotel instead of heading to her house?

Arnav tried recalling again, but the only thing he remembered was that they had a few drinks before leaving the pub. Then they took a cab for a short ride. And before he knew it, they had reached someplace. It sure didn't look like a hotel, he thought back. It was a two-story building. She had asked him to keep mum as she paid the driver, and then climbed the staircase to the second floor.

This was not a hotel, Arnav told himself and got off the bed. He needed something to get rid of the headache. Arnav walked towards the kitchen but didn't find her there. He opened the fridge; it was empty except for the milk can. He cursed under his breath and snapped the door close.

"Fuck" Arnav muttered.

I need something, anything.

Arnav then walked towards the washroom to check if she was in there, taking a shower. But as he reached there, he was disappointed to find that she wasn't there either.

Where are you?

This was new for him; it was always the other way around. Usually, he would always get up first in the morning and leave the house without waking the girl. He didn't want the girl to wake up first, he never liked it. He was not good at the conversations, especially the ones those happened in the morning.

Arnav panicked as he remembered something and rushed to the bedroom and started looking for it frantically. He checked the table for the wrappers; they weren't there. He checked his wallet; there were still some condoms in there, but then he didn't know how many were there

                    In Their Shoes

before, so he couldn't figure out if he had used them.

Arnav sat there, cursing himself again. It had happened once long ago when he had picked up a girl from a pub and done it in her car. When they had both stripped their clothes, Arnav had opened his wallet to find that he didn't have any stock. But it was too late by then to back out, so they did it anyway.

After they had lied naked next to each other that Arnav had grasped how stupid and careless he was. Arnav had made a mental note as he returned home that he would always check his wallet before leaving the house whenever he felt like going on a hunt. However, he had forgotten to make a note about keeping count.

Arnav sighed as he sat there holding his head in his hands, thinking about what had happened to that girl, as he had never seen her after that night. A part of him was happy that they had never crossed paths again, because he didn't know what would have happened or how the girl would have reacted. What if she was pregnant? He pushed the thought away as quickly as it had come. That was the last thing he wanted.

Arnav's eyes shot open as he remembered he hadn't checked the dustbin. He heaved himself to his feet before walking towards the dustbin and emptying it on the ground. He sighed as he found the wrappers there.

Arnav put the things back in the dustbin before he grabbed his clothes. His attention went to the note kept on the bedside table as he slipped into his shirt. Arnav picked it up and read it. He finally had an answer to why the girl was missing; she had gone for a morning walk. It was too early though, he thought as he checked the time. He thought of crumpling the paper and throwing it in the dustbin, but then decided against it and slipped it into his denim pocket.

Arnav made sure that he hadn't left anything before coming out of the apartment and closing the door behind him. He gingerly stepped down and was out of the premises before the owner could notice him.

It doesn't belong to me; He recalled the girl telling him as they were ascending the steps; *I stay here as a tenant. If she catches us, we will have to go back in the cab and do it there;* she had whispered in his ears and giggled.

The driver would disapprove, Arnav wanted to tell her. But before he could open his mouth and speak, she had opened the door and pulled him on herself. Her hands ran through his hair and her tongue buried inside his mouth.

She was different from the girls he had slept with before, Arnav told himself as he dwelt on last night. Some were very naive and would get tired quickly, and then some were very dominating, which he didn't like. But this girl, Arnav failed to recall her name, she knew her way. And for a moment, he thought of meeting her again. But immediately, he pushed the thought away.

Arnav walked out to the sight of people thronged around something. He stopped for a moment before walking towards the crowd. He pushed through them till he was in the circle and froze when he saw two cars rammed into each other. He looked at the girls they were trying to pull out from the one of the cars, before looking at the girl who was reporting the news – the one with whom he had spent the night. He froze for a moment when he recognised the girl. Arnav's attention then went towards the blood splattered on the ground. He felt light-headed as he turned around and walked out of the circle; It triggered memories he had tried to bury many times. He bumped into someone as his vision blurred, and with a jerk he was pulled back in his past.

Arnav was sitting on his bed, hearing the heated argument between his parents. They had got the news about the lady – whom Arnav and his mom had gone to meet despite his father's disapproval – she had taken her own life.

"Why are you doing this?" Arnav's Mom snapped at his father.

"Doing what?"

"Why are you sending him away?"

"We have already talked about this. It's the only option we have."

"We had one more option..."

"And that option has just taken her own life; she can't help him now." Arnav's dad snapped back. "She couldn't help herself; she couldn't help her son. What made you think that she could have helped Arnav?"

"She could have helped him, had you not taken her life!" Arnav's mother lost her composure.

                                              In Their Shoes

"What did you say...? What did? How come...?" Arnav's dad stuttered. "We both know she took her own life."

"Yes, but it was after you went and met her. It was you who..."

"Watch your tongue, you..." Arnav heard his father splutter before he heard something break. Arnav quickly got down from his bed and ran towards the door; luckily, this time it was not locked from outside.

There was a silence in the hall when Arnav opened the door of his room and walked toward his dad. There was a broken glass vase on the ground; next to it was a pool of blood, and his mother lying in it, lifeless.

4 - JAYESH SALASKAR

Jayesh sat in his chair absent-mindedly, drumming his fingers on the table in front of him. His eyes were on the white mark where once he used to wear the engagement ring. His mind drifted back to the days when life was normal, when he was normal. There was a wry smile on his face when he thought about her, the day he had met her for the first time. He was in a court for one of the cases he was working on, and she was representing the person they had charged.

"So, you are telling me you are too arrogant to accept the possibility that the guy might be telling the truth, that may be a mistake has been made in the police investigation?" She had asked as he stood in the witness box, her eyes looking straight into his.

She was younger than him, three or four years maybe; He couldn't tell. But she was fierce and appeared mature for her age. She was a few inches shorter than him; her light brown hair tied behind her head, leaving a few stray hairs to fall on either side of her face. He hadn't seen someone so intimidating before. The way she spoke and eyed him made him feel that there had indeed been a mistake at his end, and he had missed something in the investigation. She stood there in front of the witness box, crossing her arms, and dared him to defy her

"Yes." There was a long silence in the courtroom before Jayesh finally spoke. "There are chances of the department overlooking a fact or two."

She had turned towards the judge then, not waiting for Jayesh to finish. "I think my client should get bail on that ground."

When the judge granted bail to her client, she had simply collected her files and walked out of the courtroom. Jayesh felt like running after her but then decided against it, for he was a police officer who had filed a case against her client, and second, he had the same feelings that most guys have when they really like someone – she is way out of my league.

Jayesh's watch beeped, and he was kicked out of his past. The officers assigned to him for the night shift were sitting on their chairs, trying to fight sleep. Jayesh checked his watch as he tried to stifle a yawn himself. He felt drowsy, and his eyelids drooped. He sighed and

                                            In Their Shoes

rose as he saw that his shift was over, and his relieving officer would be on his way to report for duty.

"Shinde. *Utha,*" Jayesh said to the officer sitting on a wooden bench next to his table, whose back was resting against the wall and had just closed his eyes. He woke up with a start and looked at Jayesh, startled. Jayesh simply smiled at him and walked out of the room.

Jayesh had stopped doing night shifts after his dad had passed away as there was no one to look after his younger sister – Niyati. She wasn't a kid, but then he was a brother, and had promised his father that whatever happens he will always be there for her. His senior was kind enough when he had confided this to him and ever since had not called Jayesh for night shifts.

However, a couple of months back, when Niyati moved out of their house to stay away with her friend, Jayesh had asked his senior to re-assign him night shifts. And now, after two nights in a row, Jayesh recalled why he hated night shifts. It wasn't like Jayesh had much to do in the night shift anyway; he had to simply do some rounds of the area to make sure that the night wouldn't turn into a nightmare for people, and then get back to the station. But just sitting idle and going through files wasn't his way of working; he liked being in the field, chasing criminals.

Jayesh recalled the last time he had gone after a criminal after receiving a tip from a source, just a month after he had lost his dad. He had finished his shift and walked into the alehouse instead of returning home, despite several warnings from his fiancé that he needed to keep tabs on the drinking habit he had picked up after losing his father. Jayesh was a few drinks down when he had received a call regarding a contract killer who was in town for a kill. Usually, Jayesh would have contacted the control room, but that day he simply gulped one more glass of liquor and walked out of the alehouse and towards the location where the contract killer was supposed to be.

Jayesh had reached the spot within a few minutes, and though he was in plain clothes, the killer and his partner recognised him. Before Jayesh could pull his car over, they opened fire on him; bullets shattered the glasses of his car and punctured a few holes in the left door. One of the bullets kissed his stomach, and blood gushed out in rivulets. Within a few minutes there was a big red patch on his white shirt. He lost control of the car and bumped straight into another one. He lost consciousness before he could get control of himself.

Jayesh's team reached the spot when someone from the vicinity dialled 100 and rushed him to the hospital. X-ray had confirmed a small crack in his ribs, and he had to make sure something like this didn't happen again. It wasn't because of the bullet; the crash had caused it. And though he didn't confide in anyone, he still felt the pain intermittently. And it would shoot suddenly through his body, and he would try everything to stop himself from wincing.

Jayesh felt exhausted as he walked towards the changing room. *Maybe I am getting older,* Jayesh told himself as he walked, *or perhaps I just need some sleep, and it will be okay.* A part of him told him bluntly that it was just a lie. Jayesh stopped in front of his locker and opened it to pull out his clothes. He unbuttoned his shirt and removed it before slipping into the casual check shirt his sister had gifted him on his last birthday.

"Dada, you are getting older now." Niyati had teased him that day as they were having dinner. She had insisted they would go someplace and celebrate his birthday, but he had refused as he loved spending time at home.

"Find someone else and get married." Niyati had added as she munched on the rice. "And if you don't have the guts to ask someone, let me know; I will take the responsibility."

"I see someone is more eager than me to get married." Jayesh had quipped, looking at his sister.

"It's nothing like that." Niyati had responded as she finished her dish. She had then stood up, picked up her plate, and walked to the kitchen. He had then pulled out his phone to check if there was a message from the girl wishing him happy birthday, but was disappointed when he didn't find one. He wanted to be angry with her, but then knew that it wasn't her fault; It was him who had screwed things up.

When months had passed, and he had thought of moving on, he had tried dating other girls; But somehow, it didn't work. It wasn't as if they weren't nice, but they just weren't her. And when he realised that he was just searching for her in all the girls he dated, he had stopped it.

Jayesh closed the locker and pulled out his phone to call Niyati. He

                                                    In Their Shoes

leaned against the locker and dialled her number. It was ringing, but no one answered. When she didn't answer the first call, he dialled again and waited.

Niyati had told him last night she was going out with some friends when she had called. Jayesh would have asked her to stay home but knew she wasn't a kid anymore, and she wouldn't like him continuously telling her what to do. A part of him told him that maybe that was the reason she had moved out to stay with her friend.

"How long will you be there? Few days or a week?" Jayesh asked when Niyati had told him that she wanted to go and stay with her friend.

"Not for a few days, Dada." Niyati had clarified.

"Meaning?" Jayesh asked, even when he knew what she meant.

"I want to move in with her."

"Why do you want to live in a rented place when we own one?"

"That's what everyone does nowadays." Niyati had argued. "And I want to live my life on my own. I want to be independent." she had added when he didn't reply and simply shook his head in disapproval.

"No means no; you are too young to do that." Jayesh rose, hoping to mark the end of the conversation.

"Baba would have allowed me to do so." She had said when he had hardly taken a few steps towards the kitchen. He knew it would come to this. He paused in his tracks and sighed.

"Okay, do whatever you want." He gave up and walked straight into the kitchen.

"You are the best brother, Dada." She exclaimed as she stood up before running towards her room.

"I know, and that's why you are going to stay with your friend." He had mumbled.

Jayesh sighed when she didn't answer the call second time either. He put his phone in his pocket and walked out of the locker room. He had taken only a few steps when his phone rang.

"It must be her," Jayesh told himself as he fetched his cell. The cell phone's screen flashed the control room number.

"Hello." Jayesh reluctantly answered the call.

"Sir, we have received a call from a girl informing us about an accident."

Jayesh paused and sighed. He thought about sending someone else but then decided against it.

"Send me the location and copy Kamat as well; tell him to meet him there instead of coming to the station." Jayesh disconnected the call and put the phone back in his pocket before walking back to his locker.

As Jayesh sat in his car and checked the coordinates of the scene, he thought of quickly checking it out and then heading straight to Niyati's friend's house. He would go there and tell her that this was enough and ask her to pack her bags and return home.

A few seconds passed, and Jayesh sighed as he realised he was overreacting. If she wasn't picking up the call, it wasn't her fault, maybe the phone was on silent; after all, it was the early hours of the morning.

As Jayesh's car screeched to a halt and he got down, he saw one of the officers approaching him. As usual, crowd and news reporters had thronged the place. He always wondered how news personnel always reached before he could. *Maybe I am getting older,* he told himself.

"Drinking and driving case?" Jayesh questioned as the officer came closer, and then glanced at the cars that had crashed into each other. His eyes stopped on the Audi for a second, and he saw the medical crew pulling someone out from it. He had suffered several head injuries, Jayesh observed.

"Another rich brat," Jayesh remarked, still looking at the driver who was facing the other way, waiting to see if he knew which politician or businessman's son he was. When the guy didn't turn around, Jayesh looked back at the officer who was standing next to him.

"Is there something wrong?" Jayesh saw that the officer wanted to say something but was struggling to find words.

"Sorry, Sir, but there is..."

Jayesh became attentive to the tone of the officer. Right at that moment, someone from the crowd bumped into Jayesh. Jayesh briefly looked at the guy before turning back to the officer.

"What happened?" Jayesh asked again.

"One of the girls..."

     In Their Shoes

Before the officer could complete his statement, Jayesh looked back towards the accident scene, and saw the girl they had just pulled out from the car and put on the stretcher. He felt as if a bullet had hit him, knocking his breath out. Jayesh froze where he was, transfixed. He didn't hear what the officer was trying to say.

"NO" Jayesh screamed, but his voice never came out. Jayesh gathered all the strength he had and darted towards the ambulance.

"NO" He cried again as he saw his sister's face covered in blood. Her eyes were still open, but he didn't feel her presence in them. As he held her hand and stared at her, his mind went blank, and he felt empty. The next moment he was lying on the ground, unconscious. Though his heart was still beating, a part of him had died with her.

5 - Asmita Deshmukh

"Why on earth people call at this time of the morning!" Asmita muttered as her cell phone rang for the third time.

When it had beeped first, she thought it was an alarm; her hand involuntarily had come out of the blanket and groped for her cell before pressing a few random buttons and turning off the sound. Few seconds had passed in silence before it had beeped again. When she had reluctantly checked her phone, the screen flashed an unknown number calling. She had felt like answering but decided against it as she saw it was six in the morning. She silenced the ringer and put the phone face down. She needed sleep desperately. She had stayed awake most of last night, perusing through her client's files, trying to find a way to save their ass.

Being a lawyer sucked sometimes, as she would feel tired and exhausted by the time she went to bed, if she got the chance to sleep. But being a criminal lawyer demanded this from her, because her one mistake could cost someone life or years in prison. Asmita recalled a case where she hadn't slept for three nights in a row when the public prosecutor had provided evidence that her client was present at the crime scene, which she was unaware of. She had slept only when she had found a constructive argument to save his ass from getting into jail; she had won the case eventually.

Asmita would often find herself in a dilemma about taking a particular case, as sometimes it would become difficult to tell if the person who approached her was telling the truth and was innocent. This feeling would sometimes last even after she had accepted the case or sometimes when she had turned it down.

There were times when Asmita would think about quitting her work and doing something she had wanted to do ever since she was a kid, exploring new places. Though she hadn't checked, she knew she had saved enough money in the past few years to do that. But then, some things were holding her back. The last time she had come close to doing this was when she had come out of a relationship; she had stopped taking any cases and searched a few places she would have liked to visit. Her dad had later changed her mind.

"It's something I have wanted to do since I was a kid, and you know this." Asmita had said as she sat on the couch, next to her dad.

"Yes, I know." Her dad had responded as he gently patted her hand. *"Even your mom had the same wish; it was me who couldn't manage time for that. And now that we have time, she is not allowed to travel long distances due to her medical condition."*

There was an edge of guilt to his voice when he spoke. Asmita didn't say anything and rested her head on his shoulder.

"I had even asked her once to go alone, for I was buried till my neck in work and your brother was still too new in business for me to leave him alone to handle it."

Asmita listened to her dad and tried to understand why he was telling her all this now.

"You know what she told me?" Her Father had a trace of a smile on his face.

Asmita didn't say anything but shook her head.

"She told me there would be no point in travelling to places if I wasn't there to hold her hand." There was a long pause before he spoke, as if reliving the moment or maybe recalling the words her mother had used.

"We never talked about it again, as I knew she was right, and part of me was too selfish to let her go and live without her." Her dad said and smiled, as if to himself.

"And to be frank, my dear," He continued as his wrinkled fingers gently stroked Asmita's hairs, *"you are just trying to run away. And that, my dear, is not how you live your life."*

Asmita snapped back from reverie as her phone rang for the fourth time. She cursed her luck and removed the pillow under which her head was buried.

"Hello." She said in a half-sleepy voice as she answered the call. Her eyes were still closed, and she wished it was some marketing call she could end and go back to sleep.

"Am I speaking with Asmita Deshmukh?"

"Yes, who is it?"

She couldn't make out what he was saying because his voice was very low. But the word Soham and accident made her get up and sit upright in her bed; her sleep was suddenly gone.

"What happened? Is he okay? Where is he now?" Asmita shot an array of questions at the guy on the other side of the phone as she flung the blanket away and jumped out of the bed.

Asmita splashed some water on her face when she ended the call, and then pulled out some clothes from the cupboard before slipping into them. Asmita's heartbeat was unsteady when she closed the door behind her and walked towards her car. The only thing she had been told was that Soham had met with an accident and was in ICU. Asmita had asked for the address and told the man she would be there in no time. She had thanked him again for informing her before disconnecting the call.

Asmita climbed the steps two at a time after the receptionist told her the ICU was on the first floor; she didn't have the patience to wait for the elevator. As Asmita stopped in front of the ICU and peeped through the small glass window fixed on the door, she saw her brother lying on the bed, with various medical equipment kept on both sides. Soham's head was covered in a bandage, and the only thing she could see were his closed eyes.

"Can I meet him?" Asmita asked as the doctor closed the door behind him and told the nurse about which medicines to administer to Soham.

"Yes, you can." The doctor responded looking at Asmita as the nurse walked away. "But make sure you don't wake him up; he is on tranquilizers and needs rest."

Before Asmita could ask how he was, the doctor had left. She entered and sat on the stool next to the bed where her brother was lying.

What if something had happened to him? Tears formed in Asmita's eyes as she dwelled on the thought. *What would I have done?*

When Asmita had heard the person saying something about the accident, her heart had skipped a few beats. The last time she had gotten a call about an accident, it was about her parents; And by the time she had reached the hospital, they had left the world. Asmita had slumped against the wall and cried her heart out since she didn't know what to do.

                                                    In Their Shoes

Asmita didn't leave the house for weeks after their funeral. She had closed herself off from the world, even her brother. She didn't feel like doing anything, as if she had lost interest in living. But then, as the weeks turned into months, Asmita realised that she was being selfish, for she had completely forgotten that her brother had lost his parents too, and he was way younger than her. Few months later, when Asmita found out that Soham had started drinking, she pulled herself out of her reclusion for his sake; but she was too late, his drinking had already turned into addiction.

Asmita couldn't recall the last conversation they had when Soham was sober. She had tried speaking with him on various occasions, but somehow it never worked. Sometimes she would feel that there was something more he was going through. Maybe he had some other problems he was hiding from her.

But why? She had asked herself several times and didn't have an answer.

Asmita was sitting around the dining table, waiting for her brother to join her for breakfast. She had decided that she would talk to him today about what was wrong and why he was behaving like this. He had again returned home in a drunken stupor last night, which had become a kind of routine after their parents had died. It was about time she settled this.

A few minutes later, Soham walked out of his room and joined her for breakfast. He took a piece of bread and was applying butter when she broke the silence.

"When will this end?" Asmita asked, looking at him.

"What are you talking about?" Soham responded, behaving as if nothing had happened.

"Stop acting; you know very well what I am talking about." Asmita snapped, "I am tired of you behaving like this, returning home late at night drunk, and not telling me what has happened."

"I have lost my parents." Soham shot back, keeping the bread and knife down on the plate and looking at her; his eyes were red.

"So have I." Asmita countered, hurt.

"It doesn't look like that." Soham said as he pushed the plate away

and got to his feet.

"Where are you going now?" Asmita asked as Soham walked towards the door.

"I need a drink." Soham retorted, closing the door behind him.

Asmita was pulled out of her memories as a nurse entered the room. She rose, planted a kiss on her brother's forehead, and walked out of the ICU room.

Asmita saw few officers near the reception as she searched for a coffee machine; she needed something to get rid of the dizziness and headache. She spotted one near the entrance where a sofa lined the wall. She walked towards it and bought herself a cup of coffee.

Asmita had just taken a few sips when she saw the television and grasped why the police officers were there. The television screen flashed news of her brother's accident. Asmita felt weak in the knees and collapsed on the couch behind her as she read that two girls had died in the accident. Tears found their way out of her eyes as she read the name of one of the girls. Asmita sat there, holding the cup of coffee in her hand, trying to comprehend the enormity of what had happened in one stroke that night.

6 - ARNAV INAMDAR

"What are we, if not characters, from one story or another, playing our part, knowingly or unknowingly, willingly or unwillingly." a female voice said as if reading through Arnav's eyes.

Arnav tore his gaze from the frame hugging the wall and looked at the source of the voice. The old lady was standing next to his chair, smiling down at him. He was back in his past, recalling the memory of his visit to the old lady, the only visit, which was the reason for what he was today.

"It's a line from one of his novels, my son's." She said, as if answering his unasked question, and walked around the table, pulled up her chair, and sat down.

"Do you know who I am?" The old lady continued with a faint smile plastered on her face.

Arnav didn't say anything but shook his head. Her expression turned sad at his reply. But the expression was gone as quickly as it had come.

"Do you know why we are here?"

Arnav silently indicated no.

"Well," the old lady continued, "I am here to help you. And I cannot help you until you are ready to talk."

Arnav looked at her with a blank expression, trying to understand who she was and why his mother had brought him here when his dad was against it.

"Can I ask you some questions?" she added when Arnav didn't reply.

This time Arnav agreed.

"How often do you hear the voices?" The old lady asked, her eyes scanning his face as if he was some object.

"Every day." There was a long silence before Arnav had answered. "They follow me everywhere."

"And what do they say?" Her voice was barely audible.

"They say that…" Arnav trailed off, fearing that if he told her, then even she would think it was true; the reason why he had never told his parents about them. Or maybe they knew, and that's why they were planning on sending him somewhere.

"Go on…" She leaned forward and placed her wrinkled palm on his hand. The lines of veins were visible through her skin.

"They tell me that I am a monster," Arnav confided, tears forming in his eyes as he searched the room. His mom wasn't there.

"Do you believe them?" Her expression was suddenly changed.

Arnav didn't have an answer. He simply looked down and stared at the carpet below. She removed her spectacles and kept them on the table as she heaved herself out of her chair and covered the distance between them.

"Would you like to take a small walk, young man?" She stood next to him and pointed towards the garden on the other side of the glass wall. Arnav nodded and got down from the chair.

The old lady didn't say anything and left Arnav to his thoughts as they walked out of the room and stepped into the garden. The path they traced was covered with small pebbles, and it felt strangely good as his naked feet stepped on them. As they walked, Arnav saw pine trees lined on both sides of the path, forming a cover above their head, filtering the sunrays.

"He was the same age as you… my son," After they had covered some ground she spoke again, "when it happened for the first time. I was in the hall reading a book when I heard it. He was arguing with someone. For a moment I thought he was speaking on the phone with his friend. But I threw the book down and ran towards his room as I recalled there was no phone in his room."

She stopped and looked at him to see if he was listening.

"'You are lying,' I heard him say as I stood outside his room and tried to understand what he was talking about." She started walking again and continued.

Arnav simply followed her trail.

"'Just go away. I don't want to talk to you', he yelled. I felt as if there was someone else in the room too. I quickly unlocked the door and

In Their Shoes

opened it. He was lying on his bed, his eyes closed, and face covered with sweat. I scanned the room, but there was no one. I was clueless about what was happening since he didn't say anything while I was in the room. I walked out of the room without waking him up, thinking he must have had a bad dream."

"But I was wrong, and it happened again the next day, and the day after that." Arnav saw her expression change; But again, that look was gone as quickly as it had come.

"It kind of became a routine. I called his father, who was out of town for business and asked him to return at once. I didn't know what was happening to our son."

"We showed him to doctors once my husband returned home; even took the opinion of other psychiatrists. All of them said the same thing, he is normal; he must have had some bad dreams. But then, call it mother's intuition or anything, I knew there was something wrong." She heaved a sigh and went mum as if lost in memories.

"After a few weeks, he confided in me that he heard voices wherever he went. You know what they used to say to him?" She looked at him, "You are a monster."

"It wasn't true." She added as soon as she told him this, "I knew this then, and I know this now as well." She smiled; there was warmth in it.

Arnav didn't say anything and looked away, unsure if she was still talking about his son or him. Arnav then recalled the conversation of his parents, his dad talking about sending him away.

"He didn't want to go either," The old lady said, as if reading Arnav's thoughts.

"We had tried everything, but it wasn't working, and then one day, a friend of my husband told him about this place."

"I was completely against sending him there, but it was his dad who was adamant. There was a part of me that hated him for that, I even felt that his father didn't love him. But then I fathomed whatever he was doing was for our son; it was me who was being selfish for not allowing him to get a chance of treatment."

"He stopped speaking to us when we told him about this." She said

with a wry smile, "But we didn't have any option. We would meet him once a week; and would always find him sitting under a tree, away from other kids, in his usual place. He never talked with us during those visits; it was his way of punishing us. He had picked up the habit of reading and would spend his entire day lost in books. We thought it was just a matter of time, but we were wrong. Whenever we visited him, he would act as if he didn't know us. I don't know what it was, whether the place, or the reading habit, or the writing which he had picked from somewhere or someone, but he changed with time and became someone we didn't recognize. He was a completely different person, but the fact that he was getting better made us overlook that."

The old lady trailed off and seemed lost in thoughts, as if tired of revisiting the past.

"A few years later when we wanted to bring him back home, he told us that he didn't want to come home, and he never did. Not after months, or years, or decades. He didn't return when his dad was ill, or when he passed away. He didn't come to give me the invite when he got married, or when he had his first son. He just couldn't forgive us."

The old lady went mum again.

"Do you want to know a secret?" There was a pause for a long time before she spoke again.

"I hear the voices too." She whispered in his ear.

Arnav looked at her, wondering if she was telling the truth or lying to make him feel better and normal.

"The voices you hear aren't in the room but in your head. If you don't want to go to that place, you will have to learn to control them before they start controlling you."

The old lady looked into his eyes and ran her hand through his hair.

"You have his eyes." She looked away. "I think we are done for today; it won't be nice to keep your mom waiting for a long time."

Arnav looked to his right and saw his mom sitting on the bench there, surprised about when she had walked in and why he hadn't noticed it. Arnav then jumped down from the bench and walked towards her.

Arnav woke up and leaned back in his chair, trying to get his bearings of time, and surrounding; he was in his study room. The left side of his face had turned red and taken the mark of a file on which he had fallen asleep. He tried to rub the sleep out of his eyes and stifled a yawn as he again leaned forward. The paper cuttings and articles on various cases he was reading before he had dozed off were scattered on the table in front of him. These were the articles about cases where someone was accused of the crime but later was released after he had provided an alibi.

Arnav had written two books about alibi and was currently trying to find the story for his third. Arnav straightened up and continued perusing through the cuttings again, trying to see if any case struck him as odd. It wasn't an easy thing to do, to search for a monster when masks were getting thicker. He had found a case where he was sure that he who had walked away because of an alibi was indeed the murderer, but the crime had happened in Pune, and he didn't want to revisit that place as it reminded him of his childhood. So, he crossed it out. There was one case in Surat, but when he tried to find out about the accused woman, he found out she had died last year in a car accident.

Though Arnav had dived into the pool of papers he had in front of him, the pictures of the morning when he had walked out of that girl's house and straight into an accident site were still vivid in his memory. The voices were still fresh in his ears, as if he was still standing there again, amongst the crowd.

When Arnav couldn't erase the faces of the girls lying lifeless on stretchers and blood splattered on the ground, he simply sighed and closed the files. He closed his eyes, trying to steer away his mind from the thoughts, but failed at that too. Arnav then opened his eyes and looked at the morning newspaper perched on the edge of the table. He fetched it and read the headline of Niyati Salaskar's prayer meet. Arnav's eyes stayed on it for a few seconds before he read the address and rose.

Arnav walked into the washroom and splashed some water on his face. He walked back in his bedroom, opened the cupboard, pulled out his denims and a white shirt. He slipped into them before he walked out of his house and closed the door behind him.

7 - Jayesh Salaskar

Jayesh sat broken in a chair, rocking it back and forth as if caught between his present and past. He was sitting in Niyati's room. His one hand was holding a glass he had just emptied, while the other held a half-burned cigarette, the smoke of which had fogged his mind.

After the funeral, he had gone to Niyati's friend's place, brought back all her stuff, and arranged it in Niyati's room. On the wall in front of him hung a large square wooden frame which held their family picture; he stared at it and tried hard to believe it had all actually happened, and they were gone just like that, leaving him alone. He felt as if life was taking away the things he cared about most, one after another.

Jayesh scanned the room again. Her presence was there; he could feel it in every corner, and yet somehow, she wasn't there. On his left, above the bed, was another wooden frame. It had a picture of Niyati and her friends when they had gone on a trip.

"Had it been a one-day trip, I would have allowed it, but I cannot say yes to this. I am sorry." Their dad had reacted as Niyati talked about the overnight trip she had planned with her friends.

Niyati had then looked at Jayesh who was leaning against the door frame, and eyed him to take her side.

Jayesh had shrugged his shoulders as he decided not to intervene. Her face had turned red when she had looked back at her dad.

"What is the point of Dada being in the police force when his sister can't go for a night out?" She had protested and stormed out of the room, tears welling up in her eyes.

"I was allowed to do the same thing when I was about her age," Jayesh had said when only his dad and he were left in the room, "then why not her?"

"I know." His father had replied, "It's not like you were allowed because you are a boy, and she isn't allowed because she is a girl."

A sudden cough spasm stopped him, and he winced as his hand went for the glass of water. Jayesh quickly darted towards the bed, removed the lid from the glass, and helped his father to drink the water.

"It's just that I feel more protective of her than I feel about you." He said as he kept the glass back, *"And you know that."*

"She is like her mother; she thinks that the world is full of nice people. If you will be nice to them, they will be nice to you…" He trailed off as he recalled his late wife. The expression on his face was somewhere between wistful and dreamy.

Jayesh had few memories of his mother from childhood, but Niyati hadn't seen much of her as she died soon after Niyati was born. His father had given them the love of both mother and father. Though their dad never talked about their mother, Jayesh knew he missed her more than he or Niyati ever did. When he was a kid, he would often find his dad sitting on a chair with a glass filled with liquor and staring at his wife's photo, reliving her memories.

"And we both know how guys are." Jayesh had snapped back from reverie as his dad spoke again, *"I sometimes fear what if…"*

"Dad," Jayesh had interrupted his father as he held his hand.

"Nothing will happen to her; you are just over thinking." Jayesh assured him. *"There are other girls with her, she will be fine."*

Jayesh opened his eyes, kept the empty glass on the table next to his chair, and stubbed out the cigarette in the overflowing ashtray. The copy of the post-mortem report was still lying there on the table. His fingers brushed on the file for a few seconds before he picked it up. He stared blankly at it, fighting with himself whether to read it again or not. It was not going to change the fact no matter how many times he read it; and still, he opened it and went through it. He stopped at the line, and tears formed in his eyes.

"She was pregnant," Jayesh mumbled and closed his eyes, letting a few more tear drops roll down over his cheeks.

Jayesh held the report in his hand as he picked up the empty glass and the ashtray and heaved himself out of his chair. He knew he couldn't keep himself locked in the room and distance himself from the world, at least not today. He walked towards the study table and placed the empty glass and ashtray there before opening the drawer and putting the report in it. He then walked towards the washroom and splashed some water on his face before walking back in his bedroom and slipping into a white shirt.

Jayesh saw people gathered in the garden as he reluctantly came out of his house. Some of them were his colleagues, some his friends, neighbours, and a few distant relatives; most of whom he had seen last time when his dad had died.

"Sorry to hear about your loss." One elderly woman said, walking up to him. Jayesh didn't say anything and looked at his shoes, holding back tears.

"But sometimes it is not in our hands." She patted his hand, "Just let it go." He looked up at her and nodded.

"Take care. Don't be so hard on yourself." Her frail hand touched his face.

After she left, he stood there as everyone started coming and offered him their condolences. When Jayesh couldn't take it anymore, he simply excused himself and walked towards the place where his sister's photo was kept. As he was making his way through the crowd, his eyes met with a guy, and as soon as that happened, the guy looked away as if trying to avoid eye contact. Jayesh found it odd, but before he could give more thought to it, he bumped into someone.

"So sorry... I..." Jayesh heard a familiar voice.

Jayesh's thumb involuntarily traced the white mark the engagement ring had left behind as he recognised the face, and he was once again pulled back into his memories.

"Have you lost your mind? What were you trying to do by going there alone when you should have taken a team with you?" She asked as she stood next to Jayesh's bed. Her hands were crossed, and her face was red.

This was right after the incident when Jayesh had gone after the contract killer and ended up getting injured.

"What if the bullet..." She had trailed off when she couldn't complete the sentence and sighed, tears rolling down over her cheeks.

"I know what you must be going through after losing dad. But drinking or acting careless is not a solution to that. And just to remind you, it's not only you who have lost a father; Niyati has too."

Jayesh had no answer to this.

"Are you trying to get yourself killed, one way or another? Have

                    In Their Shoes

you ever stopped and thought about what would happen if something happened to you? How will Niyati move on with her life? how will I ..." she trailed off again and looked away.

"I am sorry," Jayesh had finally said, "I was drunk, and I made a wrong call."

"You drank again?" She regarded him in disbelief.

"It was just one..." Jayesh didn't complete the statement.

"Really?" There was an edge of exasperation to her voice.

"It won't happen again."

"You said the same thing last time." She snapped at him.

Jayesh didn't say anything and simply stared at her.

"What is it going to take for you to understand that you can't continue to act like this? As if everything is finished in your life, as if I or Niyati doesn't exist or matter to you anymore. And if that's the case, there is no point in me wearing this."

Before Jayesh could understand what she meant, she had removed the ring, placed it on the table next to his bed, and walked out of the room.

8 - Asmita Deshmukh

The day Asmita had returned home after the funeral of her parents, sat in her room, and cried, she had wished silently that life wouldn't make her wear it again. But then, here she was, wearing that same white dress and making her way through the sea of people wearing white, who, like her, had come to pay their respect to the girls who had lost their lives in the unfortunate accident.

In the morning, Asmita had gone to see her brother again, like she did every morning; She, however, couldn't speak with him since he was still unconscious due to the painkillers they were giving him. Asmita wanted to talk to him and know what had happened that night, to tell him that she was there with him, and everything was going to be okay.

The reports pulled that morning were normal, and Soham's health was steadily progressing. Asmita had kept the bouquet and get well soon card on the table next to Soham's bed and sat there for a long time, arguing with herself about whether to go to the prayer meeting or not. And then somehow, an hour later, she found herself getting out of the car and walking towards Jayesh Salaskar's house.

Asmita still wasn't sure if she should be here, as she didn't know how Jayesh would react; for it was her brother who was driving the other car and was still alive. Asmita paused in her tracks as she started having second thoughts about being here, and was about to turn around when she walked into someone.

"So sorry, I was..." Asmita trailed off and froze as she looked at the person standing in front of her. Before Asmita could gather herself, she was pulled back into memories.

"So, you are telling me you are too arrogant to accept the possibility that the guy might be telling the truth." Asmita heard herself saying, she was in a courtroom representing her first client and questioning the investigating police officer.

Asmita was fresh out of law college; the only things she had was a law degree, experience of the few cases in which she had assisted a senior lawyer, and lots of enthusiasm. This was Asmita's first shot, and she was trying everything to do her best to prevent her client from

In Their Shoes

going behind bars. Asmita had just recited the dialogue she had learnt watching serials on courtroom drama. Calling a police officer arrogant was bold, Asmita knew, or maybe plain stupid, but it had worked somehow.

Judge had granted bail to Asmita's client. She had then grabbed the files and her belongings and quickly walked out of court before the officer could catch her and snap at her. He didn't look that type though, a part of Asmita had argued with herself; she didn't know why. Despite this, Asmita did her best to not bump into that officer in every consecutive trial; she didn't want to take a chance. But then sometimes there are things which are bound to happen, and you cannot run away from them. On the fourth court date, Asmita's client was acquitted of all charges. After completing all the formalities, she was waiting for the cab outside of the court.

"You were good there."

Asmita had turned around after hearing these words to look at the source of the voice and froze when she found the same police officer standing in front of her, a smile plastered on his face.

"And a bit arrogant too." Asmita heard herself saying when she had composed herself. He had caught her off guard.

"Oh, and I thought it was only me." His reply made her smile, killing the awkwardness between them.

"I am here to say thank you, by the way." The way he looked at her made her feel something.

"For?"

"For producing the truth in front of the court and stopping an innocent from going behind bars," He offered.

"That's my job and what I get paid for." Asmita regretted it the moment she said it.

He looked down before replying, scrubbing his right shoe absent-mindedly, "Well, that matches our work description as well."

"It happens sometimes, we think of someone as something they are not." Asmita told him then, recalling her father's favourite line from her childhood.

"You are right." He said, looking back at her, "Thanks."

"You are welcome." Asmita had said and smiled before walking away, not knowing what else to say or do. She even forgot that she was waiting for a cab there.

"Hey," He had called her after she had taken a few steps. Asmita had turned around, surprised.

"I think a simple 'thank you' would make me look arrogant, and I don't want it to happen again."

"So, what are you suggesting?" She asked, fidgeting with the files she was holding in her hand, feigning as if she didn't get where he was heading.

"There is a coffee shop nearby..." He trailed off, maybe because he thought he was being too pushy.

"I will pay," Asmita had taken a whole minute to say yes when her answer was ready even before he had asked the question.

They walked for a few minutes before reaching the coffee shop, a small place with a few tables arranged in front with a small canopy covering it.

Jayesh pulled a chair for Asmita and waited for her to settle before sitting opposite her. She looked at the surroundings, twirling strands of her hair around her fingers, trying not to look straight into his eyes. Jayesh drummed his fingers as he impatiently waited for the waiter and looked at everything but her.

"Are you new here?"

The waiter had taken the order and left the table when Jayesh broke the silence.

"No," Asmita answered at once, relieved that he had started the conversation.

"I mean, I never saw you before this case. And I usually visit the court at least once or twice a week."

"Maybe you did, it's just you might not have paid much attention."

"I doubt that."

"Sorry?"

"It's okay."

The words brought Asmita back to her present, and she found

                                          In Their Shoes

herself standing a few feet away from Jayesh. If he was surprised to see her there, he didn't show it on his face. She took a step back and looked at the figure standing in front of her. His hairs were messed up, his face hidden behind the beard. He stood there expressionless; she looked in his eyes and realised he was drunk. A pang of guilt shot up in her body as she stood there and tried to find the right words to console him.

"I am sorry for your loss." Asmita's words were barely a whisper. She wanted to take a step closer and hold his hand but stopped herself, for the distance between them was much more than the space separating them. A sinking feeling that she might never be able to cover it made her feel sick. She tore her gaze from him and looked away when she couldn't look at him anymore.

"I hope they get justice, these girls and their families, and the culprit gets charged if he is guilty, even if it means my brother." Asmita wasn't sure why she said this.

There was silence after that as neither of them said anything and looked at the photos of those girls. They knew it didn't matter what happened, they were gone and weren't coming back.

Asmita sighed and looked back at Jayesh. He was still staring at his sister's photo, his face dreamy. Asmita took one last look at him, he was now the stranger she knew once, and turned around, realising her presence was making the things worse and she should not have come here.

"Do you mean it?"

Asmita had taken only a few steps when he asked the question. She stopped but didn't turn around.

"Do you mean the part about justice?" The accusation in his voice stung her. "Sometimes words mean nothing if they are not backed by actions"

"Meaning?" Asmita asked.

"Don't represent him in the court."

9 – Arnav Inamdar

"It's just another road accident in which someone has lost a life, and I believe it's not the first time that it has happened." One of the panel members answered the question of the reporter who was conducting the debate.

"Only because one of the girls who died was the sister of a police officer, and the guy behind the wheel of the other car is a businessman and brother of a top-notch lawyer, the case is being made a big issue. So that newspersons can get their bread and butter, and people get something to talk about; something they like to do when they have nothing else." The panellist was on fire.

The reporter flinched at the reply and looked in the direction of another panel member, hoping she would come to his aid.

"I completely agree with him." The lady replied. "It's an open and shut case; everyone knows this. Soham is going to be charged for drinking and driving, and manslaughter. And maybe that's why his sister hasn't taken his case."

"But our sources believe that Jayesh Salaskar asked her not to do so." The reporter added, "And we also know that Jayesh and Asmita share a past."

It was a strange claim, Arnav knew, but the possibility of it wasn't deniable. Arnav would have thought the news channel was simply making it up had he not seen Asmita on the day of the prayer meeting, having an intense conversation with Jayesh. He couldn't hear what they were talking about, but the way they looked at each told him they weren't strangers to each other.

Arnav also knew the source this reporter was talking about. It was Parul; she worked with this news channel. He had seen her at the prayer meeting, though it was just a glimpse. Arnav would have gone and talked to her if his eyes hadn't accidently met with Jayesh's. Arnav should have acted normal, and Jayesh wouldn't have even noticed him, but then Arnav remembered bumping into Jayesh on the morning of the accident as well, and in a reflex moment, Arnav looked away when he shouldn't have. He composed himself within a few seconds and had even started articulating a response to give Jayesh when he saw Asmita bumping into him, so Arnav had quietly left.

Arnav had tried and failed to understand the reason Asmita had not taken the case. A part of him that told him there was more to the story than met the eye; a coin always has two sides, it argued. Arnav considered the possibility that there was another side to this story. Or maybe it was just the writer in him that was overthinking, he thought; after all, they have the habit of creating stories when there isn't one.

Arnav gathered all the newspaper cuttings he had regarding this case as he turned off the television and put them back in the file before closing it. Maybe he was wrong; maybe his hunch that Soham Deshmukh would walk away in this case was wrong. *Perhaps I am wasting my time in it*, he surmised.

Arnav opened the drawer and pulled out the file he had been going through before Soham's case had caught his attention. Arnav continued reading from where he had left, reviewing the cases one after another, trying to think of what motive the accused could have had in each case.

Arnav spent almost an hour reading the file. But when the words on the page started blurring, he stopped and sighed, realising the Soham Deshmukh case was still running in his mind. Arnav closed the file before turning off the lamp.

Arnav heaved himself out of the chair and walked towards the bed; he removed his T-shirt and threw it on the ground before lying down on his stomach. He closed his eyes, but sleep didn't come.

There was something wrong with him, Arnav knew from the day he had known himself, but this was something different. It had been months since he had written anything and weeks since he had been to the pub. But then it had something to do with that girl as well, Parul. There was something about her that made him feel the way he hadn't even felt before.

Arnav wasn't sure if his condition was worsening, or he was getting better; he wished it was the latter. On that day, when he had returned from the prayer meeting, he had laid awake on his bed for quite some time, the way he was now, thinking about Parul. She had appeared to be a completely different person on that day, a more mature and sorted person. Arnav wasn't sure that if he had gone up and talked to her there, she would have recognised or even acknowledged him. She didn't look that type, or to put in other words, he wasn't her type. But then, a part of him argued that she had left him her number, so it meant she was interested in him, and it wasn't just a one-night stand. Arnav had then thought about calling her on that day; He had even picked his cell and punched the numbers in it but couldn't hit the call button as he didn't know what he would say. Today again, a week after the prayer meeting, he felt the urge to call Parul but stopped himself.

Arnav sighed and sat upright on the bed when he felt restless. Arnav knew he wouldn't feel at ease till he gets a closure - the case and Parul. And there was one way to make some progress on both. He got down from the bed and walked towards the cupboard. He knew if he left the house now, he would be able to reach the court before the hearing started.

10 - Parul Kasbekar

Parul's life had changed suddenly, and so had the people in her office. She felt their eyes on her as she walked towards her cabin.

"Good morning!" She heard people greeting her, those who had never bothered to look up from their desks when she used to pass by.

"Morning!" Parul responded without looking at any of them; not caring about who it was.

"YOU GOTTA BE KIDDING ME?" The voice at the other end of the phone yelled at Parul as she informed about an accident where an Audi had rammed into another car. Parul had winced and pulled the phone away from her ear. Had she been a boy, she would have felt the hands reaching out of the phone, grabbing her collar, and shaking her to make sure she was serious.

After Parul had informed the police and called the ambulance, she had called her boss; after all, it was a breaking news. It made her feel sick though, feeling good that she had finally reported a big news item for her channel when someone was seriously injured or dead. People had thronged the scene, and some were even trying to pull out the people stuck in the cars. She had thought of doing so at first, but then as she peeped in through the driver seat's window and saw blood dripping from the guy's head, she felt dizzy and quickly stepped back. She just couldn't stand the sight of blood, not even a single drop. So, opening the door and pulling out someone whose head was covered in blood was out of the question. Her hands were still shaking as she gathered her senses and called her boss's number.

"Either you are drunk or just messing with me." Parul's boss sounded sceptical as he spoke. She had told him that the guy whose Audi had rammed into another car was Soham Deshmukh, a businessman, and brother of the city's top lawyer, Asmita Deshmukh.

"I am not drunk, and neither is this any kind of joke." Parul had countered. "I am standing here at the accident site."

She could hear him jump out of bed and tell her that if this was true then this was going to be big news. She had taken a photo and sent it to him after she had ended the call. She had then waited for the cameraman to reach the spot so they could cover the news.

Parul pushed through the door of her cabin and heard it click behind her as she settled in her chair. She kept her bag on the desk in front of her and turned on the computer. Her boss had given her the cabin after she had delivered the second breaking news to her boss about Jayesh and Asmita's conversation at the prayer meeting.

"Are you sure you heard it right?" Her boss had asked when Parul had recited the snatches of conversation she had heard between Jayesh Salaskar and Asmita Deshmukh.

"Yes, as I said, I was standing there when it all happened." Parul had responded as she stood on the other side of the table, her hands resting on the empty chair in front of her.

"You are saying he asked her not to take her brother's case?" Her boss confirmed, as he loosened his tie.

"Yes," Parul answered, now slightly irritated, as she couldn't understand why he thought she was making it all up. It wasn't her fault that she was first at the accident site, and then the first to learn that Jayesh had asked Asmita not to take her brother's case. She was just in the right place at the right time.

"And I strongly believe she is not going to take the case." Parul had added when he simply stood there and processed the information she had given him, thinking about how to present it.

"Why would you think that?" Parul's boss asked her as he picked up the receiver from the cradle and punched in a few buttons.

"Because I think there is a part of her that feels her brother is guilty, and…" Parul paused; not knowing if she should say this, for she wasn't sure if this was true; after all this was just a hunch she had.

"In my office, at once!" He slammed the receiver back in the cradle as he said those words and looked back at Parul, "…and?"

"I think they have history." Parul hesitated as she said this.

"Who?" He asked, completely clueless about where Parul was heading.

"Jayesh and Asmita."

Her boss sank lower in his chair, removed the lid from the glass,

                                    In Their Shoes

and gulped down the water; The expression on his face akin to that of a person who had just hit a jackpot.

"I knew the day I had hired her that she would do wonders one day." Parul heard her boss telling the senior editor who had just entered the room.

It seemed like suddenly God had started taking an interest in her life. Things were getting better. Parul had paid her pending bills and rent with the cheque she had received as a bonus, and did some shopping for herself and her parents. She couldn't recall the last time she had done that.

Parul's parents were happy when she had called them this morning and talked about her promotion and her separate cabin. For the first time they hadn't talked to her about marriage, and she was glad about it. But then, the thought brought up the memory of that night, and Parul found herself thinking about Arnav. She then looked at her cell, the way she had looked many times since she had returned home that morning to find he had already left. She cursed herself for not asking for his number.

The ringing landline brought her back to the present. Parul picked it up and heard her boss on the other side. He informed her that she had to go to cover the hearing of the case against Soham Deshmukh.

11 - SOHAM, ASMITA

"I am not denying the fact that my client, Mr. Soham Deshmukh, was driving under the influence of alcohol. All I am saying is he wasn't the only one to do so that night. The girl who was driving the other car was also under the influence of alcohol." The lawyer representing Soham said aloud in the courtroom, making sure everyone heard him before he walked towards his assistant, who handed him a piece of paper.

"And here, my lord," Soham's lawyer continued as he turned around and walked towards the judge. "…is the report supporting my claim."

The lawyer then looked at his opponent to see if he had anything to say as the judge scrutinised the document.

"I am not asking you to not punish my client for driving under the influence," Soham's lawyer continued when the judge tore his eyes from the piece of paper in his hand, "...for he is guilty of that."

He paused for a few seconds and looked at his client, giving a dramatic pause, before continuing.

"But to punish a survivor of an accident, only because he happened to drive a more luxurious car than the other one and have survived, would not be what we call justice."

Soham stood in the box, attending two trials at the same time; one was going in front of him, and another one was in his mind.

When Soham had regained consciousness after the accident, he had found himself in a room filled with various equipment and a nurse standing next to it. When she saw Soham drifting back to his senses, she had left the room to fetch the doctor.

The doctor had checked his reports and asked Soham a few questions before turning back to the nurse and giving her some instructions. Soham would have asked the nurse about his sister had the nurse not injected him with something that made him drowsy, and before he could understand what it was, he was unconscious again.

Soham wasn't aware about how long he had been asleep when he had awoken again, but this time he was shifted to a room with less

In Their Shoes

equipment. There was no presence of the nurse nor his sister, but the bouquet and get well soon card told him she had come to visit him. Soham had then lain awake on the bed with many questions in his mind. Soham wanted to see his sister, to tell her what had happened on the night of the accident, to tell her everything that had been happening before that, but she didn't show up; not on that day, not on the following day, nor the day after that.

Soham had expected her to be there a week later, when two policemen had walked into his room as the doctor was doing the last check up before his discharge, and told him he was not going home but to jail, as he had been charged with manslaughter.

"Maybe she knows I have been charged and she is preparing for the case." Soham had argued with himself as he lay awake on the lockup floor and tried to imagine the possibility for his sister not showing up.

It had finally happened the next day, a week prior to the court hearing. He was sitting with his back resting against the wall when a constable announced he had a visitor. He saw his sister standing on the other side of the bars. She stood there with her hands folded, looking at everything but him.

Soham had been preparing for the question since the day he had been moved here, the question his sister asked every client before she took any case.

"Are you guilty?"

Soham had asked it himself several times, and yet he didn't have the answer when he found her standing in front of him. She, however, didn't ask whether he was guilty; The only thing she said was she was not going to represent him in court, before turning around and walking out of the police station.

***

Asmita made sure she was the last one to enter the courtroom, as she did not want to attract more attention than was needed, and sat in the corner of the last row. Though she had not taken her brother's case, she wanted to be present at the hearing to see how the trial was proceeding.

On that day, after returning from Jayesh's house, she had walked straight into her brother's bedroom. After she had slumped against the wall and slid down to its base, Asmita let tears find their way out of her eyes.

Asmita couldn't believe what she had walked into. She had gone there only because she knew the girl once and wanted to pay her respects. And here she was now, with a thought in her mind that her brother was somehow responsible for Niyati's death and a looming question whether she should really represent him in court. Asmita cursed herself as she held her head and cried her heart out.

Her eyes and throat dry, Asmita hauled herself to her feet and walked to the place where Soham kept the liquor. She opened one of the bottles and smelled it. She thought against it and corked the bottle, only to open it again after a couple of seconds, closed her nose, and drank a few sips. The taste of it in her mouth made her retch, but she didn't stop and took a few more sips. She, like Soham, was trying to wash away her feelings of pain with the liquor. It, however, didn't help. When she had finished the bottle, she was lying unconscious on the ground like a piece of crumpled paper.

Asmita had slept through the entire day and had a debilitating headache and sore neck when she woke up. She felt as empty as the liquor bottle that lay by her side. Her hair was a tangled mess, and her clothes were dishevelled.

Asmita had then got up and left her clothes in a pile as she walked into the bathroom. She had stood in front of the mirror after she splashed some water on her face; she had never seen someone as broken as her reflection. She stood there, staring at her puffy eyes and splotchy face for a few seconds, and then with a sudden retch, she vomited all over the floor.

When Asmita had cleaned herself and walked out of the washroom, she was still feeling sick. She didn't even have the strength left to walk to the kitchen and make herself a cup of coffee. Instead, she went into her bedroom, retrieved some tablets from a drawer, and gulped them down with water. She then flopped onto her bed, not bothering to slip into any clothes, wrapped herself in a blanket, and was fast asleep in no time.

Asmita slept for the rest of the day and the night too. When she woke up again, she had lost track of time and didn't realise she had slept through two days and a night. When she freshened up and went to visit her brother in the hospital, she found out he had been discharged and was in lockup.

She had asked her assistant to collect all the reports related to her brother's case and all information about the trial. After she had discovered the girl behind the wheel was drunk too, and confident that her brother would get cleared of the charges, she decided not to represent him in court. Because she knew too well that if she did, people would say he got away because of her, and she didn't want that to happen.

Asmita had then contacted a fellow lawyer and asked him to take her brother's case. She had provided him with all the details required to acquit her brother from the charges of manslaughter, before warning him not to disclose that she had requested him to take this case. She had instructed him to walk into the police station, meet her brother, and tell him he would like to take his case as he believed he was being framed because of his profile.

When everything was set, Asmita went to the police station to execute the last part of the play; To tell her brother she was not going to defend him. She understood it would hurt him. She knew he would feel like she had walked out on him when he needed her the most. But then, there was no other way of doing it. She just wanted this to get over so that she could sit with him and talk about everything.

"The evidence and reports provided in the court prove that Mr. Soham Deshmukh was driving under the influence of alcohol that night." The judge said once both lawyers had represented their case, "However, they do not prove that Soham Deshmukh is solely responsible for the accident."

"The court, therefore, acquits Soham Deshmukh from the charges of manslaughter and finds him guilty of driving under the influence of alcohol."

***

The judge had acquitted Soham of manslaughter charges and charged him with drinking and driving by the time he had completed his walk down memory lane. Soham saw people getting on their feet and walking out of the courtroom, oblivious of the fact that his lawyer was standing next to him with a big smile on his face.

"Congratulations!" He said when Soham finally noticed his presence.

Soham didn't say anything nor bothered to smile back.

"You are a free man." Soham's lawyer continued as he shook his hand, "You just have to sign a few papers, and I will see about the fine you have to pay for the other charges."

Soham didn't say anything but looked around the courtroom again, trying to see if his sister was there waiting for him.

"I will call you once everything is settled up." Soham's lawyer continued. Soham nodded without looking at him and signed the papers as he stepped out of the witness box.

"Thanks," Soham said as he capped the pen before walking towards the exit.

"Maybe she believed I am innocent and knew I would get cleared of the charges. She just didn't want people to think I got away with it because of her." Soham argued with himself as he descended the steps.

"Or she thinks I am guilty." Another part of him argued.

***

Asmita picked up her bag once the verdict was out and mixed with the people who rushed toward the exit. She wanted to meet her brother at once, but not here; She had some business left as well. She walked towards the nearby coffee shop and sat there, her face buried behind the newspaper, waiting for people who were coming out of the courtroom to get back their life. She saw reporters fighting for a sound bite as Soham exited the building.

"How are you feeling now that you have finally been found not guilty of the charges of manslaughter?" One of the reporters questioned him.

"Are you going to file a defamation suit?" Another reporter asked.

"If you were innocent, why didn't your sister represent you in court?"

"Or does she have a different opinion?"

Soham paid scant attention to them, called a cab, and got into it, quickly vanishing into the distance.

When Asmita looked back, she found Jayesh leaving the court; he looked like he was in a hurry. Maybe he was just trying to avoid the reporters. Asmita wanted to talk to him but stopped herself, realising it wasn't the right time to do so. There were still some reporters waiting for him when he walked towards his car. Jayesh didn't say anything but simply waved them off before getting into his car.

Asmita was watching Jayesh's car going out of view in the distance when her cell finally beeped. It was the lawyer who had represented Soham in the court.

"I owe you one." Asmita said as she answered the call.

12 - Jayesh, Parul, Arnav

Jayesh stood in a corner throughout the court proceedings as a mere formality. The arguments of the lawyers representing both sides were nothing but a blur to him.

Jayesh had filed a case of manslaughter against Soham in a flush of anger while in pain over losing his sister; it was the same reason he had asked Asmita not to take the case. But when he had found out the girl driving the other car was also under the influence of alcohol, he had accepted the reality that they were equally responsible for the accident as Soham was. And then, he knew it didn't matter what verdict the court delivered, it was not going to bring back Niyati from the dead.

Maybe that was the reason Jayesh didn't react when the court exonerated Soham. Jayesh was conscious of the fact that the lawyer was right; there was no point in punishing Soham only because he had survived the accident.

Jayesh dwelled on the thought about what would have happened if the judge had convicted Soham of manslaughter. How would Asmita have taken that news? What if Asmita had ended up hurting herself? As this thought crossed his mind, he felt a chill run down his spine.

Jayesh tried to search Asmita in the crowd, and while doing so, his eyes spotted the stranger again, the one he had seen at the prayer meet. Jayesh would have ignored him had he not recollected at that moment that this was the same guy who had bumped into him the morning of the accident, near the crash site. It was the experience of working with Policy force for these many years that made him feel that there was something odd about this guy. And before Jayesh knew it, questions started flooding in his mind.

What is he doing here? What was he doing at the prayer meet? Is he from Niyati's friend circle? If yes, Jayesh would have known him. Or is he a friend of Niyati's roommate? But if so, why did he walk away from the accident site? Is he a news reporter? But then, he doesn't look like one? And even if he is a news reporter, why did he avoid eye contact when he saw me at the prayer meet, and left soon afterwards?

When Jayesh failed to find answers to his questions, he simply thought of asking the stranger. Jayesh forgot about Asmita and followed the stranger. As he walked out of the courtroom, he was stopped by the news reporters. Jayesh wasn't interested in answering any questions, so he waved them off and got into his car. He turned on the ignition and followed the stranger's cab.

***

Parul was about to join the queue of people proceeding towards the exit when she spotted Arnav, and it brought an involuntary smile on her face. Her face suddenly lit up, and she felt a fluttering inside her stomach. Before she could stop herself from doing it, she raised her hand and waved in his direction. For a moment, she thought he noticed her, but the next moment he turned around and pushed his way through the crowd towards the exit, as if running away from someone.

Parul looked in the direction where Arnav had looked before he had paled and slipped out of the courtroom, and found Jayesh Salaskar making his way towards the exit through the people who had surrounded him. Parul was completely clueless about what had just happened. First, she wasn't sure what Arnav was doing here, and then, why it had looked like he was running away from Jayesh.

When Parul couldn't get any answers to her questions, she slipped through the crowd and followed Jayesh. Her boss had instructed her to call him once the verdict was delivered and brief him about what had happened in court, but Parul simply texted him and flagged down a cab, asking him to follow Jayesh's car.

Parul had assumed that she wouldn't see Arnav again; it's not like she hadn't tried. She had visited the pub where they had met for an entire week, only to leave disappointed every day. And now that she had finally found him in the last place she could have imagined, she found him on the run from someone, or so it seemed.

Parul's cab stopped at some distance from a coffee shop where she found Jayesh's car parked. Parul paid the cab fare and headed to a corner from where she could see Jayesh. Jayesh was sitting at a table, looking into the distance as if lost in his thoughts. When she followed his gaze, she noticed Arnav sitting at the other table, his face buried in the newspaper. Parul composed herself and took a deep breath before she walked towards Jayesh's table.

***

Jayesh drove his car at a very slow pace, making sure he maintained a distance from the cab he was following. Though their eyes had met in court, the stranger didn't know that Jayesh was going to follow him; Jayesh didn't want to lose that advantage. Jayesh slowed down as the cab he was following stopped near a coffee shop. Jayesh waited till the stranger got out of the cab and walked into the coffee shop.

Jayesh was following the stranger hoping he would return home and Jayesh would get his address. It would have made things easier for Jayesh to pull out some information about him. Jayesh would have asked someone to keep an eye on him and broke into his house when the guy wasn't home. That would have been the best way to get information about him.

Jayesh dwelled on the thought of returning home before he decided against it. Jayesh had run out of patience and couldn't leave this task for another day. He parked his car at some distance before walking towards the coffee shop.

Jayesh entered the shop and sat down at a table at some distance from the stranger, making sure he wasn't noticed. Jayesh sat there, observing each move the stranger made, trying to understand what he was up to.

Jayesh was tempted to walk up to this man the minute he got out of his car, but then stifled his immediate reaction. Jayesh wasn't sure who this guy was and how right he was about following him here. Jayesh ordered a coffee and decided to wait there to see where the stranger went afterwards.

Only a few minutes had passed when he was disturbed by a girl. It took him some time to register who she was. She was the news reporter he had seen at the accident site reporting the news. He found himself seething inwardly and wanted to ask her how they could be so ruthless in their behaviour, but then stopped himself, for he realised she was only doing her job.

"I have nothing to say to you." Jayesh said, looking at her, marking the end of conversation before she could even start.

When Jayesh looked back at the table, the stranger was gone.

***

In Their Shoes

The moment Arnav had walked into the courtroom, he knew he had made a mistake coming here; He had completely forgotten that Jayesh Salaskar would be here too. Though he could have reasoned his presence in the courtroom by saying he is a writer and just observing the case, he feared it might bring unwanted attention to him and his books. And that was the last thing he wanted.

Arnav had stood in a corner, making sure Jayesh didn't spot him, and he had succeeded too, until he spotted Parul waving at him. He was going to wave back when he saw Jayesh looking in his direction. He quickly turned around, acting as if he hadn't seen either of them, and mixed with the people moving towards the exit, not sure if Jayesh had recognised him in the crowd.

Arnav called a cab halfway down the staircase of the court. He skipped the last few steps as the cab stopped in front of him. Arnav opened the door, got in, and slammed the door shut before asking the driver to get out of there quickly. Arnav was about to give him his home address when he considered the possibility of Jayesh following him, and instead asked the driver to take him to a nearby coffee shop. His hunch was right; Arnav found out as he sat down and saw Jayesh enter the place a few seconds after him.

Arnav was trying to think of a way to get rid of Jayesh when he saw Parul walking towards Jayesh. He was at a loss, wondering why she had followed Jayesh, but didn't stop to think. Arnav used the opportunity as Jayesh turned to talk to Parul and quickly walked out of the coffee shop.

13 - Mugdha Inamdar

Mugdha stood near the door as she stared at the retreating image of her son, whom she had seen after decades.

"It's you who is responsible for everything." His words rang in her head as she closed the door and walked towards her bedroom. The bitterness in his voice stung her. She felt weak in her knees, as if she had lost all her strength.

"How do you live with yourself?" He had asked as he stood in front of her, his arms crossed. She didn't say a word; She didn't have an answer.

Until Mugdha had found out about him, about the voices he heard, she didn't know he was going through the same thing as she was. But one day, when they had gone to meet him in the asylum, and her husband was talking with one of the authorities, she had sat next to him and told him that it's okay to hear voices, as even she sometimes did. It's then he had confided in her about the dream, the one where he would see kids sitting by a lake. She discovered that the son was paying for the sins of the mother. But then it was not correct, it was not fair. He had nothing to do with it; in fact, she had nothing to do with it.

Mugdha didn't know what to do when she had learnt this. She wanted to tell her husband but didn't know how to explain it. She wished she could do something to help her son, but back then, she didn't even know how to handle the voices she heard.

"I don't want you to go anywhere near my son." Her son continued when she didn't say anything.

"But I can help him." Mugdha protested when she finally found her voice.

"You can't." Her son had snapped. "You couldn't help me, what makes you think you can help him?"

"I didn't know back then, but now I know."

"No," Her son had shot back, "I don't want him near a murderer."

Mugdha had flinched at his words and regarded him in shock.

"Seriously, how do you live with yourself?" Her son repeated, "If I

were you, I would have killed myself by now." He had added and walked
out of the house, not waiting for her response.

*Mugdha hadn't said anything and simply followed him towards
the door, tears forming in her eyes.*

*As she walked back into her bedroom, Mugdha sat on her bed. She
opened the bedside table drawer and fetched the bottle of sleeping pills.
Usually, she would take one, so that she could sleep peacefully for a few
hours, but not today. She didn't want to wake up to those voices again.
Mugdha swallowed a handful of pills before she drank some water from
a glass. She then lay gingerly on the bed and closed her eyes to dream
that day again, for one last time.*

*Theirs was a small family; Mugdha, her parents, and a younger
brother. Though she was a kid, she was old enough to notice that her
dad loved her brother more than her; after all, he was the one to carry
forward his name. Sometimes Mugdha would feel as if she didn't exist,
and even though she didn't want to, she started hating her brother for
that.*

*Mugdha remembered that Sunday, it was in the evening when her
father had told Mugdha's mother that he was going for a small ride
with Durvesh– Mugdha's brother. Her mom had insisted him to take
Mugdha as well. Her father had agreed half-heartedly as he had looked
at Mugdha.*

*Half an hour later, her father stopped the car near a lake and set a
place to sit, enjoy the evening, and watch the sun go down. A little while
later, when Durvesh had started crying, her father got up and asked
Mugdha to keep an eye on him till he returned with the bottle of milk he
had forgotten in the car.*

*Mugdha, who was still angry with her father, didn't pay any
attention and lay on the grass with closed eyes, thinking about why
he didn't love her, oblivious of the fact that her brother had spotted
a butterfly and followed it towards the lake. By the time her father
had returned and yelled, looking at his son in the water, it was too
late. As Mugdha's eyes shot open and she sat upright, she found her
father wading in the lake. He returned with Durvesh unconscious in his
arms. People in the surrounding heard her father and rushed to the lake,
towering over her father, who was trying desperately to revive Durvesh.*

When the ambulance arrived, and her father carried Durvesh towards it, he stopped to look at her, "You are a monster," He said, seething, "you don't deserve to live."

14 - ASMITA, JAYESH, SOHAM

The sun had already called it a day by the time Asmita had taken care of her business with the lawyer who had defended Soham in the court and returned home. In return for representing Soham in court, her lawyer friend had asked Asmita to use her contacts in the system and dig up some confidential information to help him with another case.

Asmita parked her car in the garage and sprinted to the house. Asmita unlocked the main door and entered quickly. She heard the door click behind her as she froze in her spot as if her legs were stuck in place. She didn't need rocket science to figure out that Soham was drunk.

Soham was lying on the dining table, his legs dangling down and one hand holding a bottle of liquor. The table cutlery was lying scattered on the ground. Asmita was completely at a loss about why he was drunk. Soham gulped the remaining liquor and threw the bottle at the wall in front of him. Asmita flinched at the sound of shattering glass.

"Oh, look. Someone is back from vacation." Soham spluttered as he sat up and glared at Asmita.

Asmita was hurt by his words, but Soham simply ignored and continued.

"Just to keep you updated, I was charged with manslaughter. Oh wait, you know that." Soham blurted, 'And I have been acquitted of those charges."

Soham got off the table, found his legs, and tried not to fall over.

"Oh wait, you know that too, I believe. Maybe that's why that expression is plastered on your face."

"We need to talk." Asmita ignored what he had just said.

"There is nothing to talk about." Soham slurred.

"There is. There are a lot of things I want to ask, and a lot of things I want to tell you," Asmita said as she stepped closer.

"Stop." Soham said, "I am not interested in what you have to say. I don't want to talk to you or even see your face. Just forget that I am here." Soham continued, "And leave me to myself."

"It's not going to happen while I am still here. Look at what you've done to yourself." Asmita said defiantly and folded her arms; "I cannot be in the same house and let this continue."

"You have let lots of things happen. You were so self-absorbed that you didn't stop and think for a moment that I can have one as well." Soham said. "You called off your engagement and ran off when he needed you most. You locked yourself in the closet when our parents died, when I needed you the most. You have always thought about yourself first, not realising that your selfish decisions can ruin the lives of those around you."

Asmita stood riveted to the spot, letting the meaning of those words sink into her soul.

"You let them drag me from the hospital to jail, and then to the courtroom. If you have let that happen, you should let this happen as well." Soham said. "I don't want any support from you, nor want to see your face."

She wiped a tear that rolled down her cheek as she took a last look at his brother before heading to her bedroom.

Soham hadn't moved from the place and was holding another bottle in his hand when Asmita emerged from her room with bags in her hand. She kept them in the hall as she walked into his room and returned with a few books he had borrowed from her, along with some of their family photos. Asmita could feel his eyes on her as she put everything in one of the bags before she zipped it shut and walked towards the door without even looking back at him.

What she had hoped to be a real heart to heart talk had, in no time, turned into an argument; and before she could make sense of anything, she was standing outside their house with her bags full of clothes and other things. Though in a flush of anger she had packed her things and walked out of their house, she wasn't sure where she would go.

Asmita walked towards a nearby empty bench and sat down, placing her bags next to her. She thought about checking into a nearby hotel, so that she could think clearly about what to do next. She pulled out her cell phone but stopped herself before she could look for a hotel. She hated staying in hotels; their food sucked, and the rooms made her feel empty and lonely. And that was the last thing she wanted now.

Asmita sat there for a few minutes, weighing her options before

In Their Shoes

she dialled a friend's number. When there was no answer, Asmita tried to think of who else she could stay with for a couple of days before she could find a place to rent. When Asmita couldn't think of anyone else, she redialled the first number, only to be disappointed again.

Asmita sat there for some time before the cold started taking its toll. She then rubbed her hands as she got up, picked up her bags, and walked towards her car. She put her bags behind the driver's seat and then got in and started the ignition. She decided to show up unannounced at her friend's home because she had no other options.

***

Jayesh remained in the coffee shop for quite some time after he registered that the stranger had left; the coffee in front of him was untouched. Jayesh felt at a loss as he sat there. He wanted to find out who this guy was but had no clue where to start. He could have asked one of his colleagues, but then he would have had to answer questions about which case he was working on. Jayesh did not want to share anything with anyone; he wanted to handle this his way. When he realised he had been sitting there for a long time, and people had started staring at him, he simply paid the bill and walked out.

Jayesh closed the door behind him as he entered his house and walked towards his bedroom, only to return minutes later with a bottle and a glass. He then flopped down on the hall couch before he opened the bottle and poured himself a drink. He took a few sips before he closed his eyes and sighed. He was exhausted and lost.

Jayesh had emptied a few glasses when he thought about the stranger again. Was he really related to what had happened to his sister, or was Jayesh desperately trying to find any link between them so he would have some purpose to live on? When Jayesh couldn't find answers to his questions, he simply kept pouring more liquor into the glass and gulping it down.

Jayesh sat there for some time before he rose and went into Niyati's room. Emotions flooded his mind as he picked up the bag in which he had asked one of his relatives to pack their family photos and things that belonged to Niyati. He returned with it to the hall, emptied the contents on the floor, and sat amidst them.

He went through some of Niyati's stuff and relived the memories which were now just photos in the family album. When he couldn't handle the emptiness deep within him, he fetched his phone to dial a number, realising he desperately needed someone to be there.

***

Asmita had covered some distance when her phone beeped. She answered at once, without bothering to look at the screen, thinking that it might be her friend returning the call.

"Hey you!" Asmita said as the line connected, "Where the hell you were? I have been trying to reach you forever."

The person on the other side was, however, silent. When Asmita didn't get any response, she stopped her car and checked the number. It wasn't her friend.

"Hello, who is this?" Asmita asked.

Again, there was no answer. Asmita was about to end the call when she heard a glass break and realised the person on the other side was crying.

"I am sorry for everything I have done and its consequences."

The person on the other side of the phone slurred, and before she registered who it was, he had disconnected the call. Asmita panicked and redialled the number, but there was no answer. She dropped the phone and hit the accelerator. She wanted to get there before it was too late.

In Their Shoes

15 - Parul, Arnav

Parul walked towards Jayesh's table and introduced herself as a news reporter, though she hadn't yet figured out what she was going to ask him.

When she had left the court, she had a hunch that Jayesh was following Arnav. However, she didn't know why. She had tried to connect the dots and find out the link, but failed, for she had little information about their lives and wasn't sure if they knew each other.

Parul took a quick glance at the table where Arnav was sitting when Jayesh told her that he didn't have anything to talk about and asked her to leave; He was gone.

Once she was out, she tried to find Arnav, but there was no trace of him; it was as if he had vanished into thin air. She had then called a cab and headed to her office. Her boss had called twice after her texts about the court verdict, but she hadn't picked up, because she knew he was going to bombard her with questions she didn't have answers for. She quickly reached the office and rushed to her boss's cabin.

"Come in." Parul's boss said as she tapped on the door. "Finally, you are here." He looked up from the document his face was buried in. "I thought they set Soham free and put you in jail instead" He grinned. It was a poor attempt at a joke. They were lame, his jokes, but then sometimes were enough to reduce the awkwardness in the room.

"Sit." He pointed towards the chair.

Parul kept her bag on the floor and sat down.

"I believe you have something very interesting to tell me apart from the fact that Soham was cleared of manslaughter charges and booked for drinking and driving." He leaned forward and waited for Parul to speak. His specs had slid down over his nose, and his naked eyes were staring at her. Parul wasn't sure if she should tell him about Jayesh following Arnav, as she didn't have a clue what that was about.

"No, there is nothing more right now."

Her boss made a disappointed face and leaned back in his chair. "I think we have wrung the *masala* out of this case." He mumbled, as if speaking to himself.

Parul's mind was trying to articulate a reply for the questions about where she had been and why she hadn't answered the phone, when he spoke again.

"There is another story I want you to cover now."

Parul sat up straighter and leaned forward to glance at the file he slid across the table toward her.

"It's a one-week assignment in Delhi." Parul heard him say as she went through the papers.

"It's okay if you are not interested." He said, as if reading her face, "I will send someone else to cover it."

"No." Parul replied at once, "I want the assignment."

Though she wanted to stay and find out about what was happening between Jayesh and Arnav, she knew she couldn't turn down this task. She had already screwed up her last assignment; she had been asked to write an article about a pub and nightlife in Mumbai, and how it's not secure for girls. How some guys use their charm and lure girls who are under the influence of alcohol and drugs into sleeping with them; one-night stands, if one must put it politely.

The task was both challenging and interesting, and she had worked with equal dedication. She would have succeeded in writing a good article had she not ended up sleeping with one of the guys – Arnav. She wasn't even sure if Arnav was that kind of a guy; Maybe he was, maybe he wasn't. Her feelings for him were crowding her judgment. After that, she had simply scrapped the plan and told her boss that she couldn't do it, though all the notes she had prepared were still sitting on her laptop.

"Your flight is tomorrow morning. I have arranged your stay in a hotel."

Parul was relieved from her thoughts as her boss continued

"Here," He slid a packet towards her, "there is some petty cash in it."

Parul picked the file and packet and rose.

"I hope you enjoy your stay there. Have a safe journey." He smiled before burying his face in a file again.

Parul turned around as she picked up her bag and walked out of the cabin.

***

After leaving the cafe, Arnav thought of following Parul and talking to her but then decided against it, and he instead returned home.

Arnav wasn't sure if Parul had noticed what had happened in the court and deduced that Jayesh was following him. Arnav wasn't even sure about what she was doing in the cafe; had she followed Jayesh? Or she was following Arnav and simply bumped into Jayesh? There was a way of finding it out, and that was by talking to her, but then if she had figured that he was running from Jayesh, she would have asked questions, and he didn't have any answers.

Arnav got home and lay on his bed, his thoughts drifted to Parul, and he wondered when he would see her again. How close they had come to making conversation when things had suddenly gone wrong and he had fled, twice. There was something about her that made him feel different. Ever since he was a child, whenever he looked at the people in his surroundings, he felt jealous of them, for he knew he wouldn't be able to be normal like them. He knew he wouldn't be able to live life the way they did.

Arnav always lived a life that kept him away from people. He never shared anything about himself with anyone, not even with the girls he spent nights with, nor did he ever ask them about their lives. Arnav never bothered asking what they did for a living, who was in their family, or what they liked. It meant nothing to him. But when he saw Parul, he felt like getting closer to her; he wanted to know everything about her, what she liked and what she didn't. For the first time he wanted someone to know more about him, about his life, as if she was the cure he was looking for.

"Love is like a disease; and it will happen at one point or another in your life." One of the girls he met him in the pub had told him as she emptied her glass.

Arnav had stood next to her and tried to understand what she was saying.

"And the person you fall in love with will be the cure." She had continued as she asked for a refill, "So when it does, do whatever it takes to get them, or else you will end up with painkillers."

She had then paused and looked Arnav in the eye, "And if you do, my dear, one won't be enough."

"You must be a doctor," Arnav had remarked as he picked up his glass.

"How do you know?" She had asked, impressed.

"One of my many talents," Arnav had answered, taking a sip from his glass.

Arnav rolled to one side on his bed, and before he knew it, he was asleep.

16 - Asmita, Jayesh

Asmita's car screeched to a stop, and she jumped out as she turned off the ignition. She darted towards the door without bothering to pull out the key or close the door. She fidgeted on her feet, tucking a strand of her dishevelled hair behind her ear a few times as she repeatedly rang the bell. When no one opened it, she rapped on the door impatiently. The door budged slightly, and she noticed it was unlocked. She rushed in, hoping she had reached in time.

Asmita entered the hall and found the floor littered with empty bottles of alcohol, family albums and photos. And in the middle of everything, Jayesh was sitting on the floor, leaning against the couch. His right hand was resting in a puddle of blood, holding a few broken pieces of glass. She stood facing him, her breath coming in short bursts. Her hands were shaking as she went down on her knees and checked his breathing. Asmita heaved a sigh of relief as she felt a hot breath on her fingers.

"Asmita, is it you?" She heard him mumble as she was about to get up and fetch the first aid box.

"Yes." She pressed his left arm gently.

Asmita returned with the box and cleaned Jayesh's cuts before covering them with bandages. She then helped him get up and sit on the couch beside her, clutching his left hand. Jayesh leaned towards her and placed his head in her lap. Asmita kissed his temple as her fingers ran through his hair, unaware that tears had started trickling down her face.

They both sat in silence for a long time before Asmita noticed that he had fallen asleep. She slowly placed his head on the couch, trying not to wake him. While staring at his sleeping figure, she remembered that she hadn't locked her car.

A few minutes later, Asmita walked back into the house with her bags and locked the door behind her. She kept them near the dining table before glancing around at the mess Jayesh had left on the floor. She collected all the albums and photos and piled them up on the study table in Niyati's room. A casual glance at the room made her feel as if Niyati was still living in the room. She stood there silently for a while, before heading back to the hall to fetch her bags.

Once back in Niyati's bedroom, Asmita sat at the study table and pulled out her client's files from one of her bags. She knew sleep wouldn't come easily, so she decided to work for a while.

***

Jayesh woke up with a massive headache the following day and found himself sprawled on the couch. He sat upright and held his throbbing head in his hands; it felt like someone was hammering on the inside. He dragged himself to his feet, made his way to the kitchen, and opened the fridge. He poured water into a glass, squeezed a lemon into it, and drained it in one go. As he placed the glass in the sink, he felt a throbbing in his right hand, like he was holding needles. He looked at his hand, saw it covered in bandages, and recalled the incidents of last night. Jayesh recollected that he had called Asmita last night, and she was here in his home.

But where was she now? Jayesh asked himself as he ventured back into the hall.

When he didn't find any trace of her there, he headed to his bedroom, only to find it empty. When he registered that she might have left early in the morning, he stood leaning against the door of his bedroom with his eyes closed.

Did she leave without telling me? Jayesh wondered as he stood there and tried to remember anything from last night or the morning; he tried to recall if she had tried to wake him before leaving this morning.

When no such memory came to him, Jayesh walked towards the main door, opened it, and found her still parked outside. He felt a strange sensation come over him as he grasped the fact that she was still in his house, and shuffled towards Niyati's room.

The right side of Asmita's face was perched on the file she had been reading; she had fallen asleep before she could finish. Her hair was a tangled mess and had fallen carelessly over her forehead. Jayesh carefully moved the files and documents away, gingerly picked her up, and laid her down on the bed, trying not to stir her up from sleep. Jayesh leaned closer and pushed away the few strands of hairs kissing her lips. He then stared at her slipping image for a minute before covering her with a blanket and locked the door behind him as he left.

***

In Their Shoes

Asmita woke up and found herself sleeping on a bed, snug under a blanket. She sat upright and tried to recall what had happened. One look around and she remembered that she was in Niyati's room. The rays of sunlight filtering in through the curtains on her left told her it was morning. Asmita checked her watch and found that it was past ten.

Asmita understood that Jayesh had moved her here and was surprised that she didn't wake up sooner. She was still lost in her thoughts when she heard a knock on her door, and the next moment she saw Jayesh entering with a cup of coffee.

"Good morning!" Jayesh greeted as he kept the cup on the bedside table and stepped back.

Asmita didn't say anything but peered at him through sleepy eyes. His hands were in his pocket, and he stared at his feet for a few seconds before he looked up and apologised for his behaviour.

"You know how I become a mess once I am drunk."

"It's okay, we all are a mess right now." Asmita reassured him.

Jayesh then stared at her bags for a few seconds before looking back at her; the question was plastered on his face, but he kept mum. Asmita was glad because she didn't know how she would have answered it.

"Thanks for showing up last night."

Asmita didn't say anything but smiled instead. Jayesh stepped back and fidgeted with the doorknob before saying, "I have to go to the office; there is this case I am working on. So, see you later."

Before Asmita could say anything, he walked out of the room and closed the door behind him.

Asmita flung the blanket away as she finished her coffee and headed to the bathroom.

Jayesh had left the house by the time Asmita had taken a shower. She slipped into fresh clothes and checked her cell. There were a few missed calls from her friend. She sat down on the chair adjacent to the study table and observed the frames which Jayesh had put back on the wall as she called her friend.

"Hey, where are you? Is everything okay?" Asmita's friend shot questions at her as soon as the call connected.

"Slow down," Asmita replied, "I am fine."

"So sorry for not picking up your call, I was in a meeting and my cell was silent. When I saw it, I returned the call, but you didn't answer."

"It's okay."

Asmita then told her what had happened and that she would be staying with her for a few days.

"I mean, if that's okay with you." Asmita added when she was done.

"Oh, shut up. You can come and stay with me whenever you want." Her friend replied instantly. "I am out now, but you will find the key hidden behind the letterbox. I will be back by evening and then we will sit and talk."

"Thanks a lot." Asmita said, relieved.

"Oh, stop it now," her friend hushed, "See you in the evening."

17 - Jayesh Salaskar

Jayesh pulled up to an empty parking lot that evening to find that Asmita had left. He got down, slowly walked towards the front door, and stooped down to fetch the key hidden under the welcome mat. Back when they were engaged, Jayesh had told Asmita about his habit of keeping the key below the mat; something told him she would have remembered and left the key there. And she had.

Jayesh left the old thoughts behind as he entered his house. The place felt empty again, with him alone in the house. He slipped out of his clothes and went straight for a shower. He ran his hands through his hair as he tilted his head up and closed his eyes, letting the water run down his face, trying to wash away thoughts of Asmita.

Jayesh slipped into fresh clothes after the shower and went to the kitchen to fetch a cup of coffee. He pulled up a chair as he walked into his room. He took a small sip of the hot coffee before setting it down on the table and opened a drawer with the case files he was working on. As he opened the file, he leaned back and took another sip, reading the pages in front of him one more time, to see if he had missed anything; something that would cast a light on new facts and help him to progress with the case.

Jayesh had been assigned this case after his senior had found out about his drunken encounter with the contract killer. The day Jayesh had resumed duty after being discharged from the hospital, his senior had summoned him and given him this file. It contained details of various suicide cases from different cities, and Jayesh had to determine if they were indeed suicides or if there was more to these cases. Jayesh had been informed that he wouldn't be assigned any other case till he submitted his report on this. Jayesh inferred it was just an indirect way of keeping him away from another drunken encounter with a criminal.

Jayesh was halfway through reading the file when his cell rang.

"Any luck?" Jayesh enquired as he answered the call.

"I think I have found something." The caller replied, "I was going through the list of names from that file, doing background checks on each of them as you had asked when I stumbled across it."

"What is it?"

"When this guy -Tejas Bhagat, took his life, one Author had been summoned by the police, under suspicion that he had something to do with his suicide. But later he was acquitted, and the case was closed as suicide. Maybe that's why it's not mentioned in our file. I would have ignored this information as well if I hadn't come across another name from the list, Baibhav Kumar, where the same thing had happened. The same Author had been summoned by the police and was later released as they didn't anything on him. As these two suicides were in different cities – the first one in Delhi and the second Bangalore – with a three-year gap between them, nobody thought there might be some connection. But now that I dug into it, I strongly believe there might be some connection."

"But then didn't the Police in Bangalore try to find out if that Author had written any book in the past, and if same thing has happened before?"

"Maybe they didn't, or maybe they did, and since he had Albi at the first case as well, they let him go – thinking it is just a coincidence. I was not able to get hold of the officer in charge of the case in Bangalore."

"I think you are right; this does look suspicious. We need to dig into this."

"I will see if I can get any more details on this."

"Do you have a profile on the Author?"

"Arnav Inamdar." There was a pause before the guy continued, "For a few years, he resided in Pune, where his parents lived. Both are dead now. His mother died in a minor accident at home; she slipped on the floor, hit her head on the edge of the table, and died of severe blood loss. Arnav was around twelve years old at that time."

"Arnav was then sent to a mental asylum where he stayed until he turned eighteen. When Arnav was sixteen, his father had visited him and asked him to come home, but Arnav refused to recognise him. His father killed himself that same night. People say that his father never came out from shock of losing his wife, and when his only child refused to recognise him, he couldn't take it anymore and he consumed a bottle of sleeping pills."

In Their Shoes

"Arnav stayed in Delhi for a few years once he was out of the asylum, and that's where he wrote his first book. He was around twenty years old when he published it. He relocated to Bangalore within a few months of the book's release and never returned to Delhi."

"He did the same thing in Bangalore; he wrote his second book there and shifted to Mumbai."

"Thanks, I will take it from here. I will let you know if I need any more information." Jayesh put his phone down on the table and turned on the computer.

"Arnav Inamdar. Writer," Jayesh mumbled as the computer screen booted up. "He is in Mumbai and presumably working on his third novel, considering he hasn't published it yet and moved on," Jayesh wondered.

Jayesh typed the name in the search bar, and a bunch of information about Arnav Inamdar popped up. Jayesh read up the same information he had received over the phone before coming across a new article. Jayesh clicked on it, and the page that opened stated that Arnav had written two novels around the topic of Alibi; about how these people, about whom he had written the novel, had killed someone, and gotten away with it.

Jayesh clicked on another article about a man named Tejas who had been cleared of a murder charge and how his story overlapped with what Arnav had written. Tejas had committed suicide within a week of the book hitting the stands. There were many theories speculated upon. Some said the book was about him, and when Tejas found out, guilt overpowered him, and he chose to end his life. Others said this was murder, just to put an ordinary novel in the limelight and boost sales. Yet another faction claimed it was a conspiracy and Tejas was innocent of the charges he had been accused of in the book, and he was killed before he could tell the truth to the world. The last lot opined that all this was just a coincidence.

Jayesh read further and discovered – as his informer had mentioned– that Arnav had been summoned to the police station and later released following interrogation; because he had denied any relation to the suicides, and his Alibi of the nights in questions were solid. The forensic reports had also supported the claims that both cases were suicide, and there was no evidence of a struggle of any kind before the person had died. The police had even re-examined the crime scenes only to return empty-handed. In both cities, the cases were closed after ruling them as suicides.

When Jayesh clicked on the article link about Arnav's second novel, he paid attention to the face of the author, which was not clear in the first article. The first one was a guy in his early twenties, clean shaved and wearing specs, but this one was without specs, and his face was covered with patches of beard and moustache. As he stared into those eyes, it struck Jayesh he had seen this guy before. It was the same stranger; the guy Jayesh had seen at the accident site, in the prayer meet, and in the courtroom. Apparently his hunch was correct, there was something up.

18 - ARNAV INAMDAR

Arnav woke up with a start and found himself sitting on a chair, his face resting on the pile of printouts he had been going through; probably the reason his neck was hurting now. He wasn't sure how long he had slept, and he didn't have any idea whether it was day or night outside. He screwed his eyes as he turned on the table lamp, trying to adjust them in the sudden light that had filled the room.

Arnav checked the time and turned off the lamp when he deduced it was early morning. He closed his eyes and tried to sleep again, the same thoughts running fresh in his mind again. A part of him was still stuck with Parul, and another part was trying to figure out why Jayesh had followed him and what he was up to. Arnav had even contemplated packing his stuff and moving out of Mumbai when he considered that Jayesh may have dug up something about him. But then, Arnav wasn't sure about that. *What if it's nothing and my moving makes things look more suspicious*? Arnav had wondered. He didn't want to attract more attention than he already had.

Arnav didn't want to leave Parul either. He had failed to push her thoughts out of his mind. Arnav had even returned to the pub where he had met Parul for the first time, only to return disappointed. Another girl had approached him and started a conversation with Arnav as he stood in the corner, staring at his glass. To his surprise, he had excused himself from her, saying he was waiting for his girlfriend. Arnav wasn't sure why he had lied. It felt strange to him, the idea about being in a relationship, but it was the first time he had not denied the possibility of it. Arnav had even thought about calling her several times, but he wanted their meeting to be casual; he did not want to come across as someone who was desperate. As these thoughts ran through his head, Arnav drifted off to sleep, and he walked down memory lane, reliving the night he had met Parul for the first time.

"You must be an author." Despite the chaos in his surroundings, the words were strangely clear, as if someone had whispered them in his ear.

Arnav didn't take his eyes off the glass in front of him, swirling the liquid absentmindedly. Why on the earth would someone walk to the corner of the bar and talk to the guy who looked like he had just risen from the grave? He hadn't taken a shower in a few days, or maybe more, and hadn't bothered to shave either; all the required traits to socialize with people.

Arnav wasn't that kind of guy, and that was far from what he wanted. He barely left his place, or his room for that matter. He spent most of his time in the room, glued to his chair, stooped over papers, scribbling away. Sometimes giving life to characters, and sometimes taking it Away. And Arnav enjoyed it; in fact, he loved it.

Arnav was so taken by his writing that sometimes he felt he was living the characters. And so, sometimes, when he was exhausted living so many lives, he would simply stop writing, lean back in his chair, and close his eyes. He would then wonder how few papers and a pen were enough to create a different world in which he could live the way he wanted. But then, there were days when he wouldn't feel like writing at all, and the silence of the room felt eerie. Then Arnav would step out of his world and into the actual one. After all, there are things that you can't really enjoy on paper.

Arnav would simply walk into some bar and hang out with random girls, specifically those in a drunken stupor. Sometimes he would end up in his house, or sometimes in the girl's. Sometimes when they couldn't control their urge, they would simply do it in the girl's car, provided she had one. But then, there were times he would wake up on the street, without any clue about what had happened; as if the last few pages of his story had been torn from the book and thrown away. But he never bothered about it, maybe that was one of the good things about being a writer, you can always start a new story and life whenever you want.

Arnav sometimes felt it was a curse, but then he just couldn't help it. Like he was a mere paper boat in the flowing river of life. Anyways, he enjoyed the ride as long as it didn't drown him, which deep down he knew would happen one day; But he didn't think about it. Arnav wasn't one who lived in the past or craved for a future; he believed in writing a page at a time and enjoyed it. It didn't matter whether it made it to the final story or not.

"I didn't know I was that bad." The voice remarked, pulling him back to attention.

 In Their Shoes

Arnav looked in the direction of the voice and found a girl standing next to him; It was Parul.

"No, not at all." Arnav replied, his eyes still on her.

Parul met his gaze and looked away, as if searching for someone.

Arnav looked back at his glass and tried hard to recall the number of glasses he might have emptied to conjure up images of someone like her and have a conversation. But then he remembered that he hadn't even taken a sip yet. It must be the neon lights that were doing the trick, Arnav thought; or maybe she had mistaken him for someone else. That happened sometimes when one was drunk, but then she looked sober. She tucked a loose hair behind her ear as she looked back at him.

"You are an Author." Parul said; this time, it wasn't a question.

"How can you tell?" He asked, not sure what else to say.

"One, I've been watching you ever since you entered the pub. You haven't touched your glass and yet you look in a drunken stupor." Parul pointed out and smiled.

"And then now," She continued as if a magician explaining a trick, "there is a girl standing in front of you trying to have a conversation, and you are still not able to discern if I am real or just a character from a book."

Arnav felt like his face was an open book, and she was reading it. Is she trying to flirt with me? He asked himself. But then the question was WHY? Arnav shifted in his chair, suddenly feeling naked.

"I am just screwing with you, I deduced that from your ink-stained fingers." She said, smiling.

"What are you doing here?" There was an edge of curiosity in her voice, "People usually come here to hang out with someone, and of course, to drink." Her eyes were on the glass, which was still untouched.

"What are we if not characters, from one story or another," Arnav, instead of answering her question, recited a phrase he had read somewhere as a child, "playing our part, knowingly or unknowingly, willingly or unwillingly."

Arnav was roused from his sleep by the distinct sound of the doorbell. For a moment, he thought that he imagined it, for it was very rare that somebody showed up at his place. Arnav opened his eyes and struggled to find the lamp before he turned it on. He tried to rub the sleep away as he checked the time; it showed a few hours past noon. Arnav sat there and waited for the bell to ring again, to be sure if there was indeed someone at his door. When the bell rang for the second time, he gathered up his papers and put them in the locker before getting to his feet.

'Who is it?' Arnav wondered as he walked towards the door.

Arnav froze when he opened the door; His fear somehow had materialised into reality.

"I am Jayesh Salaskar." The person on the other side of the door introduced himself and pulled out a badge.

"I work in the police department. Would you mind if I come in?" Jayesh added as he looked past Arnav and glanced inside; As if scanning the room and searching for something.

"Sure." It was some time before Arnav responded, and reluctantly moved aside to let Jayesh in. He shut the door and followed Jayesh into the hall.

"Nice place." Jayesh commented as he scanned the room before he looked back at Arnav.

Arnav didn't say anything but simply nodded, still trying to figure out what Jayesh was doing here.

"I am working on a case, and I needed to talk about it." Jayesh explained.

Arnav motioned for him to sit down on the couch as he settled in the chair, still struggling to find words.

"I was going through some suicide cases that happened in the past few years which were suspicious and was trying to see if we had missed any angle in the initial investigations." Jayesh continued when Arnav didn't say anything.

"To see if it was indeed a suicide, or a murder which had very cleverly been made to look like suicide."

"What does this have to do with me?" Arnav asked, trying not to betray the fact that he knew Jayesh had seen him at the prayer meet, in the courtroom, or the fact that Jayesh had followed him after the court trial, "I mean, how can I help you with that?"

 In Their Shoes

"I have read your novels, and I couldn't help but think that there is some connection between these suicides and your books."

Arnav inhaled slowly and straightened up in his chair, not liking where the conversation was heading.

"In both the cases, the person committed suicide within a few weeks of the novel being launched." Jayesh continued.

"You are not the first person to say that Mr. Salaskar." Arnav put a fake smile on his face.

"No doubt about that, there must be a number of people saying the same." Jayesh examined Arnav. "Otherwise, why would you have shifted from Pune to Delhi, then Delhi to Bangalore, and now to Mumbai?"

"If you have searched this much about me already, officer." Arnav met his stare, "Then you would have also found out that I have been declared innocent. And I am not on the run; I like to travel to new places."

"I know." Jayesh replied. "I have read the police reports and closing statements. These cases were closed declaring that the guys killed themselves when guilt took over them, and even I had thought the same, until..." Jayesh paused and scanned Arnav's face.

"I came across another case, an old one; The suicide of a person who had lost his wife in a minor accident in the home. His only son was mentally unstable and had been sent to a mental asylum from where he vanished. And when he couldn't face the loss of both the family members, he simply ended his life."

"The report stated that the lady slipped on the wet floor and hit the corner of a table before hitting the ground. Did she? Or was someone else was responsible for her death, and got away with murder after projecting it as an accident?"

Arnav froze in his chair.

"What if the man was somehow responsible for his wife's death and his son had seen it? Or what if it had indeed been an accident, but the kid blamed his father for it? What if the man had not committed suicide, but his son had killed him after he had fled from the mental asylum?"

Arnav felt the silence in the room closing on him from all directions.

"Are you asking me if I killed my father?"

"No," Jayesh replied, "I am telling you."

"That's just a speculation."

"Not if one has CCTV footage of neighbourhood shops. It shouldn't be that difficult to prove that you were out that night."

Arnav wasn't sure if Jayesh was bluffing.

"Are you here to arrest me?"

"No." Jayesh nodded.

"Then, what are you here for?"

"I am here to know the reason for your presence at the prayer meet and the court proceedings."

There was a long silence before Arnav answered.

"I knew Niyati."

19 - ASMITA DESHMUKH

Asmita slammed the door behind her as she entered the apartment and stomped off towards her room, oblivious to the fact that her friend was sitting on the couch in the hall and staring at her in complete disbelief.

Asmita threw her bag on the bed and flumped in the chair next to the study table once she was in her room. She held her head in her hands and exhaled.

"Looks like someone had a very bad day at the office."

Asmita was relieved from her thoughts as Charuta walked into her room and sat down on the bed facing Asmita.

Asmita didn't move, nor did she care to reply. It had been a week since she was staying with Charuta, but she hadn't had any luck with finding a residence on rent. It had turned out to be a more difficult task than Asmita had thought. She had gone to visit the estate agent she had hired as he wasn't answering her calls.

"Hey. I was about to call you," The estate agent said with a fake smile plastered on his face when he saw Asmita entering his office. Asmita wanted to kick him but smothered her feelings.

"I am sorry I couldn't take your call. Please have a seat." He said, motioning towards the chair.

"No thanks." Asmita had responded. "I was passing by, and since you were not answering my calls, I thought I should drop by and check if there is any progress."

"There are few flats currently up for rent," The agent answered "however the problem is they don't want single people. But don't you worry, I am still trying and will ring you the second I have something in hand."

"Are you going to say anything? Or we are just going to sit here till this gets awkward."

"Apparently people don't rent their flats to single people." There was a hint of exasperation to Asmita's voice.

"No luck in finding a house on rent?"

Asmita dropped her shoulders as she looked up at her friend and nodded.

"See, I have already told you that you don't need to look for another place. You can stay here as long as you want."

"And if it is going to make you feel better, you can pay me rent." Charuta added, "And I have no policy regarding single tenants. Nor would I raise an eye if you brought a guy home or girl for that matter."

They both smiled before Asmita walked towards Charuta and hugged her.

"Thanks a lot."

"Common. What are friends for?. And yes, what is your plan for the evening? We could go out and eat. I don't remember the last time we did that." Charuta asked.

"Sounds great. Let me freshen up and quickly change into something else, and then we can leave."

"No," Charuta clarified. "Not now. I mean, get fresh and take some rest. I have some work which needs to be taken care of first. I am leaving now and will text you once I get free."

"Fine." Asmita eased down on the bed, "Just don't make me wait like the estate agent."

"And you better unpack this." Charuta pointed at Asmita's bags as she was about to turn around and leave the room. "It makes me wonder who is more messed up, you or this room."

***

Asmita felt relaxed once she was out of the shower and into some fresh clothes. She then walked towards the bags she hadn't unpacked yet, realising she had no other options. It wasn't like she hadn't thought about doing this before, but then she had assumed that she would move into a rented apartment within a few days; So, she had simply pulled out her few clothes and left the rest of the things untouched.

Asmita emptied the bag with all her clothes on the bed, dividing them into her casual and office clothes. She arranged everything on the shelves before she opened her second bag. It had some family photos, books, and files about cases she had fought or was currently working on. She kept the files of closed cases in the lower drawer of the study table, arranged the photos wherever she found a place, and kept the books and files of the case she was currently working on in a separate pile on the study table. Once everything was done, she stood in a corner with her arms crossed and sighed.

Now that everything was done, and she hadn't received any text from Charuta, she decided to go through the files of her client. Though she hadn't taken any cases ever since Soham's accident, there were still some old pending cases. And she was glad there was still some time for her to prepare her argument before the next hearing of these cases.

Asmita sat down on the chair and was fetching a file when she noticed a diary amongst the books which she was sure didn't belong to her. She stared at it for a few seconds, recalling if she had seen it before. Maybe it belonged to Charuta, Asmita thought. But then she was sure it hadn't been there before she had unpacked her things, so it meant that she had pulled it out from one of her bags. When she couldn't trace the source, she simply opened it and tried to read what was written inside.

The diary had records of the personal events of someone's day to day life. After Asmita had turned a few pages, she realized the diary belonged to Niyati Salaskar.

20 - JAYESH, ASMITA

Jayesh gulped down the remaining liquor in his glass and kept it down on the table, motioning the waiter to refill it. It was his fourth, the number of times he had called Asmita, or the number of times she hadn't picked up his call, the way he put it. It was his birthday, and life had thrown another new year at him.

A fresh start to live your life in a different way, Jayesh's dad would always say.

Jayesh reflected that his father was different from his friend's father. He was more of a practical guy, and always lived his life the way he wanted, without bothering about what someone would say or think. And that's how he had raised his children, Jayesh and Niyati. What Jayesh remembered of him, there wasn't a single memory of his dad in which he had regretted any decision he had taken.

"It's not the things you did in life that will make you feel sad or incomplete on your deathbed," Jayesh's father had said as he took his last breath, "but the things you didn't do."

Jayesh's father had said and smiled weakly, looking at Jayesh and then his sister, Niyati. She was holding his wrinkled hand, tears trickling down her cheeks. Their dad was always worried about Niyati, and Jayesh knew it when he found out about his cancer. She was like her mother, caring and soft-spoken, the kind who always ends up getting hurt.

"Will you do something for me?" Jayesh's father had said, looking into his son's eyes, his voice barely a whisper. Jayesh remembered trying to make sense out of his words.

"Take care of her." He had added as he looked at his daughter.

"I will." Jayesh had promised, tears welling up in his eyes, but the person on the bed never heard it.

"Sir." The waiter said as he filled the glass.

Jayesh took a few sips before he put the glass down and redialled Asmita's number and waited, somehow knowing that she wouldn't answer. When she proved him right, he put the phone back in his pocket, paid the bill, and walked out of the pub.

***

Asmita sat riveted in place as she read the last entry in the diary. She closed her eyes and held her head in her hands as she tried to believe what she had just read. The diary revealed not only that Niyati was dating Soham, but also that she was pregnant.

"Why?" Asmita asked herself. "Why didn't he tell me anything? Was this the reason he was behaving so weird?" These questions thronged Asmita's mind.

When she felt restless, she walked into the washroom and splashed some water on her face. She looked up at her reflection and suddenly wondered if Jayesh knew about this, about Niyati's Pregnancy.

Asmita went completely blank as she weighed the possibility of it.

"And if Jayesh knew that Niyati was pregnant, does he know who the father was? Had Niyati told her brother everything, or she had kept it a secret like Soham had kept it from Asmita?"

"If so, there wouldn't be a way for Jayesh to find out?" Asmita told herself.

She felt weak in her knees and stumbled backwards as she thought about it.

"What if it is the other way around? What if Soham is completely unaware of Niyati's pregnancy? What if I didn't pick up the diary from Soham's room, but from Niyati?"

The world spun around her. The fact that it was possible that one person knew everything from the beginning, and the other was kept in the dark sent a chill run down her spine. Asmita tried to think and failed to decide which one it was? *Is it her brother? And if so, why had he never talked about it? Or is it Jayesh, and if so, then why didn't he talk about it either? Was it the reason he had filed a manslaughter case on Soham despite knowing the other girl was drunk too? Was that the reason he had asked Asmita not to take Soham's case?*

The only way Asmita could find out was to talk with them, but then the question was which one to confront, as she wasn't aware which one knew, and which one didn't. Asmita walked out of the bathroom and sat down on the bed, holding the diary in her hand, turning the pages as she tried to recall where she had picked it from. Then she suddenly noticed that there was a page that had been torn out from the diary.

"What was on it, and why is it missing? Has Niyati removed it from the diary or someone else; Maybe the person who had read this diary apart from Niyati? Was there something on it that the person didn't want anyone to find out?"

When she couldn't carry the weight of the questions in her mind any longer, she grabbed her coat, phone, and car keys and left the apartment. Asmita decided to talk to her brother first; it was the only thing she could think of at that moment.

Asmita quickly got into her car and hit the road as she fetched her phone to call her brother. She noticed that she had several missed calls, a few from her friend and a few from an unknown number; the number that belonged to Jayesh.

Asmita dialled Soham's number and waited.

"Pick up, you idiot." Asmita muttered under her breath as she turned a corner.

A few minutes later, Asmita pulled up to a halt near their apartment. She turned off the ignition and had just opened the door when she heard the gunshot. She froze for a moment, and then darted towards the door realising what had happened. Her hands were shaking as she came up to the door and rummaged her jacket for her key. She opened the lock and sprinted to Soham's bedroom.

She was too late, Asmita registered as she stopped next to the bed. Soham was lying in a pool of his own blood, lifeless. The gun in his right hand told her that he had shot himself.

Asmita should have felt tears running down her cheeks, but instead, she felt nothing. She stood there, staring at her brother's dead body as she pulled up her phone and dialled Jayesh's number.

"Soham." Asmita murmured before a flood of thoughts filled her mind.

"Had I not left the house that day, had I stayed and talked with him, Soham would be alive today." Asmita told herself.

Asmita's phone fell from her hand as she went numb, and before she could understand what was happening, she was a crumpled mass on

                    In Their Shoes

the floor.

***

Jayesh had just parked his car and was heading into his house when his cell rang. He thought for a moment about whether to take the call when the screen flashed 'Asmita calling…'

"Hello." Jayesh said as he answered the call.

"Soham." There was a pause before he heard Asmita's voice.

The way she said it, Jayesh knew something was wrong. Before he could say or ask anything, the call had disconnected. Jayesh redialled her number, but her cell was switched off. Jayesh headed back to his car and started the ignition.

Twenty minutes later, Jayesh pulled up in front of Soham and Asmita's house and walked inside; he found Soham lying in a pool of blood, and Asmita lying unconscious on the ground.

21 - SOHAM DESHMUKH

"There are always other options like adoption."

Soham was no longer paying attention to what his doctor was saying.

"You can also look for a donor who will - you know what I mean..." The doctor continued.

Soham simply nodded and got up, not bothered that the doctor hadn't finished. He was here for a second opinion and to confirm that what the first doctor and reports had told him was true.

"Thank you for the suggestion, Doctor. I will think about it." Soham said and walked out of the doctor's cabin.

Soham needed some time to be alone before he faced anyone. He was still not able to believe he would never be able to become a father. He would never have someone who would survive after him and keep his name alive. Soham fetched his phone and dialled Asmita's number. He heard it ring, but nobody answered. Maybe she was still angry about what had happened at the breakfast table that morning. It was his fault, Soham told himself; because it was he who was acting weird instead of sharing everything with Asmita.

But then Soham just wanted to get a second opinion before he confided in Asmita that she would never become an aunt. And now that he was sure, she wasn't answering his call. Soham gave up when she didn't answer the second call either. Soham then thought about calling his girlfriend - Niyati, but next moment decided not to. Soham wanted Niyati to be standing in front of him when he told her about this, to see her reaction, so he got in his car and drove to her house.

By the time Soham was standing in front of Niyati's house, he had decided what he was going to do. He was going to tell her about the reports, and if he found even a trace of doubt on her face about the future of their relationship, he would break up with her right there. And, if she accepted him the way he was, he would disclose their relationship to Jayesh and Asmita, and then propose to her for marriage. And if she is ready, they would adopt a kid.

When nobody opened the door after three bells, Soham produced

In Their Shoes

the copy of the key Niyati had given to him so that he could sneak into her apartment whenever he wanted without disturbing Niyati's roommate. Soham opened the door and entered quietly before closing it behind him. Soham walked towards Niyati's bedroom when he didn't find anyone in the hall or kitchen. However, there was no sign of her in the bedroom either.

Soham sighed and sat on the edge of the bed before he dialled Niyati's number. He walked to the study table when she didn't answer the call, to see if she had left any note for him. As he was rummaging through the documents and files, something fell to the ground. It was a document that had been kept hidden inside one of the books. He opened the envelope and pulled out the paper. It was a medical report confirming Niyati's pregnancy; Soham froze.

Soham put the report back in the envelope before opening the book he had found it in. It caught his attention that the book was a diary. If only he had not opened it and read it, things would have been different today; If only. But Soham opened it, and went through the entries, one by one, only to stumble across entries where Niyati talked about the random guy she had met in a pub and the guilt she felt for cheating on Soham, even if it meant only for that instant and that everything had happened under the influence of alcohol. Soham felt weak in the knees as he tore the page from the diary and stumbled back before flopping down on the bed.

A few hours and drinks later, he found himself sitting in a pub, on a chair, a few feet of distance from where Niyati was sitting with her friends, unaware that this would be the last time he saw her alive, and he would be the one who would end up killing her.

Soham tossed and turned in his sleep as he tried to run away from imaginary figures who were closing in on him in the dark. Once or twice, he felt a cold hand on his neck trying to strangle him. Was it a hand or a sling around his neck that was getting tighter, he couldn't tell. He struggled for breath. The night was cold, and yet his face was covered in sweat, and so was his body. He tossed and turned again in his sleep, and the scene around him changed. Soham found himself standing in the witness box, all eyes set on him as the judge delivered the verdict.

"Guilty."

"No." Soham screamed in his sleep.

Though the scream was loud, there was no one in the house to hear it, nor anyone outside the house or in the vicinity. The house was a two-story apartment, built on the outskirts of the city where his parents had once lived. The road in front of the house continued a few meters and then split in two. Cold breaths were coming out in puffs from the mouth of a beggar who lay fast asleep on the bench, completely oblivious of what was happening in her surroundings. The streetlamp next to the bench flickered, trying to fight the darkness; the remaining streetlamps were already dead. The night was quiet, except the intermittent whining of dogs. One bicycle passed the bench and turned towards the left as the beggar pulled the blanket over her face.

Soham woke up with a start and sat upright in his bed. As his eyes adjusted to the darkness that filled the room, he felt as if he wasn't alone.

"Who is there?" Soham demanded, straightening up.

No one replied. Soham's hands trembled as he tried to spot the lamp and turned it on. He skipped a heartbeat as he saw a hooded figure standing in a corner, staring down at the ground, one hand in a jacket, while the other held a gun.

"Who are you? And what are you doing here? And how did..." Soham spluttered before trailing off.

The figure didn't reply, but simply pointed a gun at him.

"What do you want?" Soham gathered whatever strength he had left in him.

"The truth.".

"About?" Soham asked, though he had an inkling of where the conversation was going.

"That night of the accident."

"I have already told the truth in the court."

"Have you?" The hooded figure questioned, flashing the gun again. "What about the fact that you and Niyati were dating, or the fact that she was pregnant, or the fact that you were the father of that child."

Soham sighed and dropped his shoulders. He realised who the hooded figure was and how that person knew everything.

                                              In Their Shoes

"What do you want?"

"I simply want you to tell me the truth." The hooded figure responded.

"Yes, I killed her." Soham broke down, giving up to the guilt, knowing his time had come.

"I killed both of them." Soham confessed. "When I saw the distance between our cars getting closer, I went for the brakes, but before I could hit them, I saw the number plate and registered whose car it was. I just couldn't control the feelings and anger I was trying to stifle. And involuntarily, I put my foot on the accelerator." Soham went mum.

"I did not want to kill them, believe it or not." There was a pause of a few minutes before Soham continued, "But then sometimes we end up doing things we didn't mean to."

"Is that what you tell yourself every night before you go to bed?" The hooded figure asked.

There was silence before the hooded figure spoke again, "There are two ways we can do this. There is a gun in the drawer next to your bed, you can shoot yourself, or I will do it myself and tell your sister everything about what you have done."

Soham thought for a moment before he opened the drawer to pull out the gun.

"One more thing, I have made sure that if I don't walk alive out of here tonight, the package with your little deeds will be delivered to your sister, just in case you are thinking of shooting me."

Soham closed his eyes and tried to gather his courage as he brought the gun to his temple. The hooded figure had left the house before Soham pulled the trigger.

22 - Parul, Arnav

Being a news reporter wasn't an easy job; the week she spent in Delhi attested to that fact.

By the time Parul's flight had landed in Mumbai and she had returned to her apartment, she was feeling like a corpse, almost dead. Every inch of her body was tired and begging for sleep. She threw her bag on the table, slipped out of her clothes, and headed straight for the shower, relishing the lukewarm water running over her body.

Parul's flight was supposed to land before eleven O'clock, but it got delayed; And as if that was not enough, she had to struggle for a cab as she stepped out of arrivals. When she had somehow managed to get one, she got caught up in traffic. She had lost track of time by the time she reached home.

"It's not the glamorous and interesting job you think it is." Parul's dad had reacted when she had announced what she wanted to do with her life. "There are other interesting things to do instead of prodding into someone's life or chasing people for a sound bite."

But it wasn't enough to change Parul's mind. She had grown up watching her father and always wondered how awesome his job was. Everyday brought something new, every night he went to sleep not knowing what he would end up working on tomorrow. It seemed better than the lives of people who worked in private companies, always going to bed with the burden of the work they were supposed to do the next day.

"It's your life, and you are free to do whatever you want." Parul's father gave up, throwing his hands in the air, "Just don't say I didn't warn you."

Parul had smiled and hugged him then. But as the years passed, she learned that it wasn't her father but his experience talking that day; And experiences never lie.

Parul turned off the shower, wrapped a towel around her as she came out of the bathroom, and walked towards the kitchen. She poured some wine into a glass and was about to check what was left in the fridge for dinner when she heard the doorbell. Parul headed to the door, certain it would be her landlady. No one else would show up at her door this late; She barely knew anyone here.

Parul peeked through the door peephole and couldn't believe her eyes. She didn't remove the safety chain and slightly opened the door. Arnav was standing in front of her, as if he had walked straight out of her thoughts and materialised into reality.

"I think I knocked at the wrong time." Arnav remarked, his eyes fixed on her hair, which were still damp from the shower.

"Yes, I mean, no." Parul stuttered. She was so puzzled to see him through the peephole that she almost forgot that she had just stepped out of the shower and only had a towel wrapped around her. "I was about to slip into some clothes when you knocked."

"Well, I will wait outside till then."

"There is no need for that." Parul removed the chain, opened the door, and made way for him to enter.

Arnav quickly walked past her towards the couch, pushing away the thoughts that had started racing; he knew he wouldn't be able to deny them too long. Parul lingered near the door for a moment as she closed it behind her, and then walked towards him. Both stood facing each other, struggling to find words to start a conversation.

Parul had so many questions she wanted to ask him. She wanted to know what he was doing in the court. Had he come there to meet her? If so, why did he behave as if he hadn't noticed her when she waved in his direction? Or was he there for some other reason? Why was Jayesh following him? What was going on between them?

On the other hand, Parul also wanted to tell him that she had missed him terribly for the last few weeks. Parul instead kept mum as she was angry; he had not called her even when she had given him her number. A part of her was happy too since he had finally shown up. But she didn't know why he was there. Maybe he had forgotten something and was here to retrieve it? She tried to untangle the mixed feelings and failed miserably.

Arnav stood there, trying to find the right words to express his feelings for her. He felt an urge to tell her what a mess he was and how he desperately wanted her to come into his life and help him sort it out.

Arnav wanted to confide in her that he couldn't think about anything else but her.

When both failed to find the words, they simply stepped closer, and their lips touched. She held his face in her hand and kissed him. It was a slow and passionate kiss.

A few minutes later they were in her bedroom; Arnav moved closer to Parul till she was up against the wall. Arnav brushed her lips with his thumb as his eyes searched hers. He tucked the strands of stray hair behind her ear. His fingers caressed her right cheek as their tongues met. His left hand removed the only piece of clothing she had on, and then moved down on her left breast, gently making circles on it. Her hand trembled as she opened the buttons of his shirt, removed it, and flung it on the ground.

"Oops. I think I broke something." Arnav said, breaking the kiss; He had knocked down the alarm clock from the bedside table while trying to move Parul towards her bed.

Arnav stooped down to pick up the clock.

"It has stopped working." Arnav remarked, pressing some buttons on the clock as he picked it up. "How does this even work?"

"Will figure it out later," Parul responded as she took the clock from his hands and kept it back on the table. He pushed her onto the bed and let her unbutton his denim.

***

An hour later, as Arnav lay awake on the bed with Parul asleep next to him, he found his thoughts drifting towards his conversation with Jayesh Salaskar.

"I knew Niyati; we had met in a pub once." Arnav lied, "She was with her friends and had mistakenly spilled her drink on me. She then initiated a conversation, and we ended up talking for an hour when I mentioned that I was a writer. She was a really nice person."

"And that morning, when I was out for a morning walk, I ended up at the accident site; And that's how I found out she had died." Arnav continued. "I was at the Prayer meet to simply pay my respect like everyone else."

"Why did you try to avoid eye contact and leave then?" Jayesh

                                    In Their Shoes

questioned.

"I didn't." Arnav lied again. "There must be some misunderstanding. I left the prayer meeting quickly after offering my prayers as I hardly knew anyone."

"And what were you doing at the court hearing then?" Jayesh inquired.

Arnav paused for a moment, contemplating what to tell him.

"Let me guess. Went to see if Soham walks out free from the court?" Jayesh continued when Arnav didn't say anything.

"That's how you like a case to end, right? Culprit to walk away free, so that you can play your little game and take their lives."

Arnav kept mum.

"Well, you are going to play your little game again, this time for me."

Arnav eyed him with a blank expression.

"I want you to kill Soham Deshmukh."

"What?" Arnav was baffled. "Have you lost your mind?"

"Niyati was pregnant when she died." Jayesh ignored Arnav. "And Soham was the father. And I have a hunch Soham did it when Niyati denied an abortion."

"How do you know all this? Don't you think it's far-fetched?" Arnav questioned.

"I read it in her diary, about Niyati dating Soham," Jayesh said.

"Can I have a look at it?"

"No. I don't have it anymore."

"Where is it now?"

"I don't know. I think I misplaced it somewhere".

"Even if for a moment we assume that whatever you are saying is true, it still doesn't justify what you are asking for me to do." Arnav asked. "And how can you be so sure that Soham indeed is behind the accident and death."

"That's why I want you on this one. This is your forte, isn't it" Jayesh responded.

"What if I don't want to play this game of yours?" Arnav considered it for a moment before speaking again.

"Then the information of all your little acts will end up on one news reporter's desk," Jayesh warned as he turned around to leave, *"Parul Kasbekar, her name is, if I am not wrong."*

"What happened?"

Parul's half-sleepy voice pulled Arnav out of his thoughts. He turned his head to the left and met her eyes.

"Nothing." Arnav smiled as he kissed her nose, before pulling her closer and closing his eyes.

***

The sound of the doorbell stirred Parul from her sleep next morning. She rubbed the sleep from her eyes as she checked her watch; it was sometime past nine. It was the first time Parul had slept for this long. Parul stifled a yawn as she sat upright, came out of the blanket, and slipped into Arnav's shirt which was lying on the ground. She tied her hair in a knot above her head.

Parul looked at Arnav who was still asleep and then she walked out of the room. It was after Parul had opened the door and seen her landlady standing in front of her that she had realised her mistake; but then, it was late.

"You were still sleeping?" She remarked. "Today is not a holiday, are you alright?" she added before Parul could articulate an answer.

"I have taken the day off today." Parul replied.

"Is that a guy's shirt you are wearing?" The landlady remarked as she put on her specs.

Parul was struggling with words when she heard footsteps behind her, and before she could stop him, Arnav was standing right next to her.

"What happened?" Arnav asked, looking from the old lady to Parul, oblivious of the fact that she was the landlady.

By the time Arnav had registered his mistake, the landlady had asked Parul to pack her bags and find another room within a week. She then glared at Arnav, murmured something, and walked away.

In Their Shoes

23 - JAYESH SALASKAR

Jayesh sat slumped in his chair, staring at the ceiling above, his fingers steepled under his chin.

Though Jayesh was sitting in his office, in his thoughts, he found himself standing outside the ICU room, peeping in through the glass window at Asmita, who was lying in the bed, asleep. She had finally regained consciousness, though she had not yet completely recovered from the shock of losing her brother.

Jayesh had slowly pushed through the door and walked in before he pulled up a stool and sat next to her. She just blinked as she recognised him, but didn't say anything, and then again turned her head to look away.

It was after some time had passed in silence, as Jayesh sat there holding her hand, that she had looked at Jayesh and spoke with whatever strength she had. Jayesh was stunned as she told him about the diary assuming he didn't know anything. She told him that she was standing right outside their house when she heard the gunshot, about how she feels responsible for what happened to Soham, that he would have been alive had she not left the house.

Asmita then suddenly fell silent. Jayesh sat there and simply stared at her as he wondered about the possibility of Asmita noticing Arnav leaving the house. Jayesh's heart almost skipped a beat as he panicked at the possibility that she would trace Arnav and find out it was Jayesh who had asked him to do so. He forced his mind to steer away from these terrifying thoughts. He sat there for some time pondering about telling her everything, that she didn't know everything about her brother, and he got what he deserved, but then knew it would bring no good. When Asmita had dozed off, Jayesh walked out of the ICU and the hospital.

Jayesh blinked and found back his conflicting thoughts. In front of him, on the desk, lay Soham's post-mortem report, which he had just finished reading. It had concluded that there were no signs of struggle, and Soham had succumbed to the bullet wound. It was suicide; it's just that the investigating team had not found the reason yet, and nor they were going to find anything, Jayesh was sure of that.

The team which had searched Soham's apartment after the body had been moved for post-mortem didn't find any evidence pointing towards the presence of anyone else apart from Soham. Soham had not left behind a note stating the reason behind his suicide. Now that it was done, and the case was going to close as a suicide, Jayesh felt that the justice had been served. But the hanging sword that someone might trace back to him bothered him. The only key between someone and him was Arnav, and Jayesh knew he must do something about the author. It didn't matter what the reason was, Arnav had killed people and was a murderer. Jayesh just wasn't sure how he was going to get him.

"Sir."

Jayesh snapped back to attention and looked at the officer standing in front of him.

"While searching Soham's house for a suicide note, we came across some documents." He continued as he slid the evidence bag towards Jayesh on the table.

"There are some medical reports with Soham Deshmukh's name on it."

Jayesh leaned forward and opened the evidence bag. He then retrieved the envelope in it and pulled out the report. Jayesh leaned back in his chair and sank lower as he read Soham's medical report, the one saying he would never become a father. Jayesh suddenly felt numb, trying to believe what he had just read.

"You think this is the reason why he shot himself?" Jayesh looked up at the officer and asked when he saw that the officer was staring at him.

"There is more to it." The officer said as he conjured up another plastic bag and slid towards Jayesh on the table.

Even before Jayesh had leaned forward and picked the bag, Jayesh knew what it was. Jayesh slowly opened the bag and pulled out the piece of paper.

"It looks like a page from a diary." The officer continued as Jayesh held the paper in his hand. "We are not sure to whom it belongs. We searched the house but couldn't find the diary it was torn from."

          In Their Shoes

Jayesh asked the officer to leave before he started reading the entries.

***

I am pregnant.

I am sitting in my room holding the report which I have already read thrice. I want to believe there is some mistake with this report, but then I know there isn't, because the pregnancy kit is backing the report. Finding out you are going to be a mother is probably one of the best feelings in the world; maybe only if you are married, maybe not, I am not sure. I am not sure about how Soham is going to react either. Will he be happy? What about Dada? Will he still regard me the same way he did before or like everyone else he will also judge me?

***

There is something continually nagging me, and I am not sure with whom I should discuss it. It's about the father of the child. I know I shouldn't think about this, but there is a part of me which thinks it's not Soham. There is something I have never told anyone, not even Kyra — my friend and roommate, as I am not sure how I am going to justify what I have done. It was a mistake, a terrible one, I know, for which I am not going to forgive myself no matter what the circumstances were. I don't feel like talking about it right now.

***

I don't know what I will end up doing if I don't confess to someone. I just want to talk about it, even if there is the possibility that what I am assuming is completely wrong and Soham is indeed the father. Even if it is false and Soham is the father, it is not going to change the fact that I have cheated Soham and spent a night with someone else.

***

I had met one guy in a pub; we had gone there to celebrate Kyra's birthday. I didn't want to go that day, and I had told Kyra the same, and now I wish I had stayed home. We had fought again, me and Soham, and I was in no mood to leave the house, or even my room for that matter. Things weren't the way they used to be. His behaviour had changed suddenly. Lately, every single talk we had would end in a fight. Maybe it had something with me insisting that we tell Dada and Asmita about our relationship. He was scared that Dada would not agree with it as Asmita had called off their engagement. I couldn't convince Soham that it won't happen, because I knew Dada and how much he loves me; I know he wouldn't oppose it.

***

I was drunk that day, and there was this guy standing next to me, trying to start up a conversation. I don't remember how it started, but a few minutes later we both walked out of the pub and went into the parking lot, before I unlocked the car and got in. The next thing I remember is we were kissing each other as his hand ran down over my breast before he removed my clothes, and I followed suit. When we were both naked and he rummaged through his jeans for protection, I thought about slipping into my clothes and walking out, for I knew it was wrong and I didn't even know who the guy was. But before I could act, he had pinned me down and I knew it was too late to back out.

***

I still don't know what to do. Kyra has just called me and asked to be ready because she has planned to go to the pub again. I don't feel like going, but I know she doesn't take no as an answer. For a moment, I felt like telling her about the pregnancy on the call, but then I stopped myself; first, I want to tell Soham about it, about the pregnancy, about that night, everything. I want to tell Dada as well, since I don't want to hide anything from him anymore. I think I heard the door unlock; Kyra is here. Maybe tomorrow I will gather some courage and talk to Soham and Dada about this. I just somehow need to pass this one night.

In Their Shoes

24 – ARNAV INAMDAR

Arnav had stood in the corner and waited for his father to empty half a bottle of liquor before he had revealed himself. After they had served dinner in the asylum, and everyone had gone to sleep, Arnav had snuck out and entered his family apartment. His father was sitting on the chair next to the dining table in the hall. He looked like a person who had lost everything in life and had no enthusiasm to live on.

"Why did you?" Arnav questioned, as he looked into his father's bloodshot eyes.

His father stared at the blurred image standing next to his chair, and screwed his eyes, to see if indeed there was someone or he was just dreaming again. For a moment he felt like his son was standing next to him, but then he had just met him at the asylum, and he had refused to recognise him. So, it couldn't be Arnav, his dad deduced and looked back at the glass of liquor before taking a few more sips.

"Why did you kill her?"

"I didn't." Arnav's father responded, figuring that Arnav's voice was his guilty conscience, "It was an accident, we were having an argument, and I raised my hand and she tried to push me off."

"Directly or indirectly," Arnav cut him, "You are responsible for her death, for everything."

"You are a monster. You don't deserve to live." Arnav's father heard the voice again, hissing near his ear.

Arnav then put a couple of sleeping pills in the glass and kept the remaining tablets next to the bottle.

"Drink." Arnav said before he turned around and walked out of the apartment the way he had entered.

The doorbell rang, and Arnav snapped out of his past. As he sat upright on the chair, he figured that he was dreaming again. Arnav got up and headed to the door. He opened the door and found Parul standing in front of him, along with her bags on either side of her.

"Hey there!" She chirped as she stepped closer and embraced him.

"Come in." Arnav gestured to her as she let go of his arms. "I will take care of the bags."

Arnav's eyes stayed on her back as she walked in. She scanned the hall and sat down on the couch. Arnav brought the bags inside, closed the door, and joined her in the hall.

They both talked for quite a long time before Parul asked where the kitchen was; She was hungry. Arnav showed her the kitchen before he walked back into his study room.

After dinner, Arnav showed Parul his bedroom and told her to adjust his stuff as required. Arnav stood leaning against the door, his hands crossed, as Parul tried to clean the mess he had created. It was less about clearing the mess and more about creating space for her things. As she arranged his clothes on one side of the cupboard, before opening her bag and pulling out her clothes, Arnav mulled over whether he did the right thing by asking her to move in with him. He recalled the scene when she had sat on her bed, holding her head in her hands after her landlady had asked her to pack her things and find a new house. A part of him felt guilty, as he knew it was his mistake. Suddenly, before he could stop himself, he had told her that he would love it if she moved in with him.

"There is space for two, and anyways I am tired of living alone." Arnav recalled the exact words he had said and regretted them the moment he had said them. It's not that he didn't want to live with her, in fact he had started loving her presence in the room; He just wasn't sure if he was ready for her moving in. But as he stood there and watched Parul arrange her clothes, he knew it was too late to back out.

Arnav walked out of the room, retrieved some water from the kitchen and sat on the couch as he sipped the water.

Arnav wasn't sure how he would break the news of him moving to some other city and the reason he would tell Parul if he decided to do that. He wasn't sure if she would come with him, or it would be the end of the relationship even before it had started. And it wasn't the only problem; it had been a long time since he had published anything. And he had already used most of the money he had received from his last book. He didn't want to trouble Parul for money.

Arnav had experimented with the idea of writing about Soham's case, but then scrapped the plan. He knew it was too risky, and the

In Their Shoes

chances of Parul finding the link were way too high. He had then decided that he would change the way he worked or wrote books. Arnav wanted to change the way he lived his life; He was tired of running to new places, running away from the noose he knew was hanging above him and one day would be around his neck. And, he had even felt it around his neck the day he saw Jayesh Salaskar standing in front of him. Arnav was glad things hadn't turned out worse.

Arnav then thought about doing something else to supplement his earning, maybe a day job, so that he could continue his writing in the night. This way he would get some time to think about what he should write, or if he should even continue writing.

"What's in here?"

Arnav snapped to attention at Parul's voice and looked over his shoulder where she was standing in front of his study room.

"Nothing." Arnav answered at once as he rose, and was swiftly standing between Parul and the door before she could turn the knob and open the door.

Her eyebrows rose as she regarded him in surprise.

"Let me at least have a look and see what mess you have created in there."

"There's nothing in there." Arnav said, touching her hand on the knob, before slowly taking it in his hand.

"Really? Then what's the problem with me having a look."

"Because I have another girl locked in there, and I don't want her to find out about you." Arnav joked as he grabbed her by the waist and pulled her closer. His head leaned forward as he planted a kiss on her cheek and his left hand slid down.

"You just want to get in my pants, right?" Parul pulled her face away from his as he lifted her up and walked towards the bedroom.

"Yes, I want to get into your pants," Arnav answered as he laid her down on the bed. "But then, I also want to have kids, which will call you Mother and I Dad," He added as he looked into her eyes, meaning every word he said.

Parul looked at him longingly for a few seconds before she pulled him over herself and kissed him.

25 - Arnav Inamdar

Arnav found a day job in the alehouse as a waiter within a few months. He had searched for many jobs online, and even given some interviews, but they simply didn't work out. He was under-qualified for most of the interviews he attended. One day he had walked into the alehouse and read a notice pinned on a wall about the vacancy for a waiter. Though it was on the outskirts of the city, it was the only place which had shown interest in hiring him, and it paid him well.

The alehouse was owned by an old lady, who inherited it after her husband died. She had told Arnav about him one night, when there were no more customers and Arnav had cleared the dishes from the tables. When her husband had died, she had thought about selling the place, but she didn't know what she would do after that and where she would go, for she didn't have any children, nor did she want to live the rest of her life at an old age home.

"I will let you take this alehouse when I am gone." She had added, placing her frail palm on Arnav's arm, "Just as a backup in case your writing thing doesn't work out. Or else you will be free to do whatever you want with it."

Arnav knew she was searching for the son she never had in him. Arnav had told her the truth about being a writer and that the profession wasn't paying him enough. She reminded him of the lady he had once met in his childhood.

"Well, it seems like I will have to wait a few more decades for that." Arnav had quipped as he helped her out of the alehouse. "You don't look like a person who will die that easily."

It was past twelve now, and there were now only two tables that were occupied. Arnav delivered the order of the first table and walked towards the second to take the order. When he had taken their order for beer and was asking if they wanted any food, he heard the old lady calling him. Arnav glanced over his shoulder and froze when he spotted Jayesh Salaskar looking at him.

"This gentleman wants to talk to you." The old lady informed Arnav before she went back to her business.

Arnav stood there for a few seconds before he turned around and walked towards the counter; He gave the order details before he finally looked at Jayesh, wondering what had brought him here at this hour.

"Can we?" Jayesh requested, pointing to an empty table in the corner, and walked towards it without waiting for Arnav's consent.

Arnav followed him and pulled up a chair to sit. They sat facing each other for some time before Arnav broke the silence.

"Why are you here?"

"Relax," Jayesh responded as he fetched a bunch of papers from his bag and put it on the table, "I am just here to return the favour."

"A Favour?".

"Yes, for what you did for me, I thought I ought to repay you in some way."

Arnav looked at him, confused.

"I hope you have not already started writing the third instalment of your book series." Jayesh continued as he pointed to the papers. "Or else the weeks I have spent typing this draft would be a waste of time."

Arnav stared at Jayesh for a few seconds before he looked at the bunch of paper and pulled it towards him. Arnav opened it and flipped through a few pages.

"I have tried my best to copy your writing style." Jayesh continued.

A few pages in, and Arnav cottoned on that the story wasn't about Soham killing Niyati and walking away but was about Arnav. The story revolved around Arnav and the people he had coerced into killing themselves.

"Why?" Arnav looked up at Jayesh and asked, as he perceived where this was heading.

"This." Jayesh responded as he slid the torn diary page towards Arnav.

Arnav picked it up before he read it.

"It's a page from Niyati's diary," Jayesh continued, "It's about a guy she had met in the pub; the one she had spent the night with, the one she thought was the father of her child when she found she was pregnant."

Jayesh paused and let the words sink into Arnav's mind.

"I now know why you were trying to avoid me. You were the father of her child." Jayesh said when Arnav looked up at him, rage flaring up in his body.

"You are responsible for Niyati's death. You are responsible for everything that has happened."

Arnav looked at Jayesh for a few seconds without uttering a word, before he looked at the bunch of papers and placed his hand on it, "how does it end?'

"The way it has always ended," Jayesh pushed the chair back and rose, "with life.

***

An hour later, Arnav stood outside his apartment as he rang the bell, his mind still occupied with papers Jayesh had given him. On his way from the alehouse to his apartment, Arnav had pondered about what he was going to do with it. Arnav was unable to understand what was going on in Jayesh's mind. He was not going to arrest Arnav, he was sure of that; nor was he going to kill him, because if that was what he wanted to do, he would have done so by now. He was up to something, which Arnav couldn't fathom.

Arnav also considered moving to some other place, somewhere far away where Jayesh wouldn't find him. But then, what would he say to Parul?

"Hey!"

The door in front of Arnav opened and Parul's chirpy smile freed Arnav from his thoughts, for now.

"You haven't gone to sleep yet" Arnav remarked as he entered.

"I still have some work I need to finish." Parul responded, avoiding eye contact as she closed the door and followed him in the hall.

"Really?" Arnav asked as he slouched down on the couch, searching for the files and papers, usually scattered on the table next to the couch. The files were closed, and the papers were kept in a pile. He didn't say anything further and simply waited for her to meet his eyes

"Okay, you got me." Parul gave in when their eyes met, and then

                                          In Their Shoes

sat next to him as her hand moved through his hair before she planted a kiss on his cheek.

Arnav wrapped his hand around her as she rested her head on his chest and kissed her head.

"I cannot sleep without knowing you are home." Parul confided in him then.

"I know." Arnav smiled, thinking how lucky he was to have someone like her in his life.

"And you are getting thinner with each passing day too." There was a long silence before she spoke again. For a moment, Arnav thought that she had fallen asleep.

"So, I want to make sure that you are not skipping dinner." Parul added as she looked up into his eyes and then got up.

"But I never skip dinner." Arnav argued as he grabbed her hand in time and stopped her from heading towards the kitchen, "Even if I have to have it for breakfast."

"Really?" She smiled coyly as she tried to free her hand.

"Really." Arnav responded before he pulled her on him.

Arnav lay back on the couch, his arms straining her, not allowing her to let go. She simply gave in and got lost in his eyes. He tucked the stray hair behind her ears and pecked her nose, before moving down to her lips.

"If you don't want me to be awake and open the door for you when you return home," Parul said as they broke the kiss, her hand still running through his hair, "why do you ring the bell despite having a spare key?"

She wriggled herself free from his arms as Arnav struggled for a reply.

"Get fresh, I will serve dinner." Parul added and then walked to the kitchen.

Arnav got up and walked towards his room.

When he returned to the hall, she had set the plates on the table, and was sitting on the couch.

***

"Sometimes I feel as if you are a completely different person, someone I have never met. And it bothers me." Parul said as they lay awake on the bed after dinner, entangled in each other.

"What makes you feel so?"

"There are many things I don't know about you. You never talk about your family or relatives."

"I don't have any relatives." Arnav answered without any trace of emotion, "And I lost my parents when I was a kid. So that's why I never mention them."

"I am sorry for that." Parul embraced him tightly.

"It's okay." Arnav responded, his facial expression unchanged.

"On that day when I was about to enter that room," Parul continued, "you stopped me, and the look on your face was completely different, as if I had caught you in something."

"It's just a room where I write." Arnav replied, "It's a complete mess in there because I haven't cleared it in years. I didn't want you to judge me looking at it."

Though the answer didn't satisfy her, she moved on and asked the next one.

"Why was Jayesh Salaskar following you on the day of the trial?"

"I seriously don't know. In fact, it had completely slipped my mind," Arnav reacted, "but now that you have reminded me, I will go and ask him first thing in the morning."

Parul didn't say anything but simply looked at him, wondering whether to believe what he was saying.

"You have stopped drinking ever since we have started spending time together."

"Well, at least you can put that in the positive things column." Arnav quipped, his finger tracing an imaginary line on her right shoulder.

"I am serious." Parul pulled herself up from him and stared at him.

Arnav sighed, and his expression turned serious.

"I have a monster locked in a cage within my thoughts, and when I drink, it's like giving the wheel in his hands. And I don't want that to happen when you are around me."

"Really?" She touched his cheek and made him look at her, "So

                                                    In Their Shoes

you're telling me you have two monsters, and I haven't met the second one?"

"It's not a joke."

"Well, I would like to meet him." Parul said, playing along, as if they both were reciting some part of his novel.

"Let's hope it doesn't come to that."

"Why not? I might talk him into something. And if it doesn't work, we always have the option of putting a bullet through him and freeing you from his clutches."

"You do understand that you might end up killing me in the process?" Arnav remarked, pained at how casually she had said it.

"Well, what use will you be to me, if you are not you?"

It wasn't the way she said it, but the way she held his gaze that sent a chill down his spine and made him shudder.

26 - Parul, Jayesh

Parul tried and failed to recall when she had been this happy and content with her life as she sat in a cafe and sipped her coffee. She was happy about the fact that she had finally found someone who cared about her and loved her the way she loved him. But then, when you find everything going well in your life, you either question if it's all real, or find yourself thinking something bad is going to follow it.

Parul closed her mind to the passing cloud of thoughts and dialled her mom's number. It had been a week since she had talked with her. She was in a dilemma about whether to tell her about Arnav and the fact that she had finally met someone with whom she wanted to settle down and spend the rest of her life with.

Even though Parul wanted desperately to tell her parents, as they were worried about her future, she felt like she was rushing things. She wasn't sure how Arnav felt about their relationship, and if he would be okay with taking things a step further.

"Hey *beta,* how are you?" Her mother's voice disrupted Parul's ponderings.

"I am good, Aai." Parul replied, "How are you and Baba?"

"We both are good."

There was a silence as Parul debated whether she should bring the topic of Arnav, or at least tell them she was seeing someone.

"It's been a long time since we have seen you." Parul's mom continued when Parul didn't say anything.

"Even I miss you both and want to meet you; but it's just that I am stuck with work."

"I know, and that's why your dad and I have decided to come and meet you."

"No." Parul replied at once and straightened up in her chair.

"Why?" Parul's mom sounded hurt.

Before Parul could articulate a reply, she saw Jayesh Salaskar walking towards her table.

"Mom, some work has come up. I will call you later to talk about it.

Bye. Love you. Take care."

Jayesh was standing next to her when she ended the call.

"I am Jayesh Salaskar."

"I know who you are." Parul cut him off.

"Oh, I completely forgot this is not the first time we are meeting." Jayesh remarked, as if to himself.

Parul was at a complete loss about what Jayesh was doing here, when he asked if he could join her.

"I have nothing to talk about." Parul replied, recalling the exact words he had said to her.

"Are you sure? What if it's about Arnav and why I was following him that day?"

Parul didn't say anything, and Jayesh simply pulled up a chair and settled in it.

"How much do you know about Arnav?" Jayesh asked.

"I am sorry, I don't understand your question." Parul replied, confused about where this conversation was heading.

"I mean, how long has it been since you have known him?"

"A couple of months, why?"

"How much do you know about his past?"

"If you are so interested in knowing about it, why don't you ask him?"

"I have, and that's why I am here." Jayesh responded, "He is not the guy you think he is."

Parul sat frozen in her chair as Jayesh informed her about Arnav's first two books and how the men on whom he had written the books had committed suicide. Jayesh explained to her how he had walked away due to Alibi each time. Jayesh then told her that he believes that Arnav has also killed his own father, and It's Arnav who is behind Soham's death as well.

"I had seen him at the accident site, and then at the prayer meet, and again at the court; that was when I felt suspicious for the first time, and that's why I followed him that day. And had you not interrupted, I would have got him, and maybe Soham would have been alive today."

Jayesh continued.

"The day I had found Soham's body, I knew it was Arnav who had done it, but there was no point questioning Arnav on this as I know that he will produce an Alibi." Jayesh lied, 'And something tells me that it would be you."

Parul didn't say anything.

"Was he with you on that night?" Jayesh questioned.

"He was." Parul answered reluctantly.

"And can you confirm how long he stayed there?"

"He visited at night and left in the morning."

"At what time at night?"

"I don't know." Parul responded.

"Wait.. I think somewhere around one o'clock" Parul recalled the time she had noticed on the broken clock as she had kept it back on the bedside table.

"You sure?"

"Yes. Why? At what time did Soham die?"

"Somewhere around Two," Jayesh answered.

Parul felt relieved at that, just for a moment though. Because the next moment, she recalled that Arnav had showed up at her apartment unannounced. And before that, he hadn't even tried to reach her even when he had her contact. Parul felt a cloud of doubt hanging over her.

"I still somehow feel that he is connected to Soham's death." Jayesh remarked. "I still think he is guilty."

"And why should I believe you?" Parul asked.

"I am not asking you to do that. I will leave it up to you to find the truth about him. I am just here to warn you." Jayesh said as he rose from his chair.

"Stay safe. And yes, I need your permission to keep a guard near your house for your safety."

"Not needed, I am safe with him."

Jayesh stared at his shoes and sighed.

"If you don't want a guard, can you at least keep this for your safety?" Jayesh said as he cautiously produced a gun.

"Just until you are sure about Arnav." Jayesh added when he noticed Parul's hesitation. "You can return it to me after that."

Before she could say anything, Jayesh laid the wrapped gun on the table and walked away.

***

Jayesh spent the rest of the evening with Asmita, and after they had dinner and Asmita had retired to sleep, Jayesh left his apartment again.

A few minutes past twelve, Jayesh entered the alehouse where Arnav worked, and found him sitting in the corner, lost in the papers on the table in front of him.

"May I?" Jayesh said as he walked up to the table, pulled up an empty chair, and sat across the table, without waiting for Arnav's reply. Arnav straightened up in his chair.

"Working on the new novel," Jayesh remarked as his eyes strayed to the scattered papers.

"Why are you here?" Arnav asked, ignoring Jayesh's comment.

"I had one question, I thought I would come and ask you," Jayesh answered.

Arnav looked at him, blankly, trying to figure out where this conversation was going.

"What would happen if someday someone finds out about you, about what you have done? What if that mask falls from your face and someone sees the monster that lies behind?" Jayesh continued as he tore his gaze from the papers in front of him and looked straight into Arnav's eyes. "Especially someone who loves you unconditionally."

"I don't understand," Arnav said.

Jayesh rummaged in his jacket and produced a piece of paper from his pocket. "I am here to tell you how it's going to end."

"What is this?" Arnav looked at the piece of paper Jayesh was holding.

Jayesh slid the paper across the table towards Arnav. "It's an Alibi— well, not literally. But you will find out soon enough what it means."

Jayesh then took a last look at Arnav, and slowly pushed back his chair, got to his feet, and walked out of the alehouse.

27 - Parul, Arnav

Parul sat in the cafe for a long time, trying to make sense of what Jayesh had revealed to her before she finally got to her feet and returned home.

Parul shut the door behind her as she entered the house and stormed into Arnav's study, the room he had stopped her from checking out. The room was a complete mess, the way Arnav had remarked she would find it; maybe the only truth he had ever told her. The room was quite small, cramped with a computer perched on a wooden desk, with a printer next to it in one corner. Next to it was a wooden table with a small lamp on it. In front of the table was a single chair.

Parul walked towards the table and found it littered with various newspaper cuttings of the Soham Deshmukh case. Parul kept the articles aside and opened one of the drawers. As she went through the files in it, she noticed they had information about various cases where the prime accused had walked away due to Alibi. Parul opened the second drawer and came across few more such articles and the research Arnav had done on these cases. Jayesh wasn't lying; Parul cottoned on as she kept the cuttings back in the drawer.

Parul opened the third drawer and froze; it had some pictures of Soham with other girls. She closed it when she could no longer look at them. She then opened the last drawer and pulled out a bunch of papers with Alibi written on the first page. She held the papers in her hand but couldn't get herself to read it here. Parul feared about what else she might find out if she stayed any longer in this room. She then walked back to the hall, poured herself a glass of liquor, and sat down on the floor. She drained the glass before she could find the courage to read what was written on the papers.

An hour later, Parul sat broken on the couch and looked vacantly at the lopsided photo she had tried to remove from the wall; she had given up, realising she wasn't left with the strength to remove it.

Parul faintly remembered Arnav taking this photo on their first night; It was after they had made out when Arnav had pulled her closer and bit her ear – or pretended to do so. She had pulled the sheet over her body in time before he had clicked this picture. She had almost forgotten about this until she had moved in with him and he had shown her the printed copy. It was intimate – both - the moment they had shared and the fact that he had kept it with him as a memory. But when she was going through his stuff couple of hours earlier, she had opened one of the drawers and found many such pictures – in somewhat similar positions with different girls. And suddenly, it made her feel like a whore.

The pages of the manuscript she had just waded through were scattered everywhere on the ground. Parul turned off the light and lit a candle on the table in front of her before turning on the music system.

The manuscript had revealed everything about Arnav; about how he made people kill themselves, and then walked away with an Alibi. It also revealed the truth about Arnav and Niyati, about how Arnav was responsible for everything – from Niyati's pregnancy to Soham's death. Parul also figured out that now that he had killed Soham, he would soon move away to some other city, leaving her behind; to kill some other person, to cheat some other girl, to collect one more trophy.

"Why?" Parul mumbled, and tears ran down her cheeks as she perceived she was just a character in the story he had plotted. She recalled the incident with a watch on that night when Arnav had shown up at her doorstep – the same night when Soham had killed himself. Arnav could have easily set the time while picking up the clock from the ground. She didn't notice it afterwards as the clock had stopped working. But now that she thought about it, it made sense. It wasn't an accident. Arnav had simply used her as an Alibi so that even if they traced Soham's death back to him, he would walk away scot-free.

"Why? Why me?" Parul cried, feeling used and cheated.

I wouldn't let this happen again, I wouldn't let him ruin someone else's life, Parul assured herself.

Parul sat there for quite a long time, as if a dead body, holding the gun in her left hand which Jayesh had given her for her safety, hidden below a pillow. She was so lost in her thoughts that she didn't hear the bell, or the cell which flashed 'Arnav calling'. The screen went dead for a few seconds before it flashed back to life.

Parul didn't move when the door was unlocked and Arnav entered the house.

"You are still awake." She heard Arnav say as he lit a new candle and kept the lighter back on the table. She didn't answer or move. Her eyes were still staring blankly at the photo. When Parul didn't respond, Arnav walked towards the wall to adjust the photo.

"How do you feel when you kill someone?" Arnav had hardly taken a few steps when she finally found a voice, "I mean in your books." Her question stopped him.

Parul rose and walked towards him; he was staring at the papers on the floor.

"Do you feel guilty? Or you tell yourself that you did what needed to be done?"

Arnav was still staring at the papers, with his back towards her. A few seconds passed in silence before he turned around. His eyes strayed to her bare legs before falling on her face. Parul searched his eyes but didn't find the Arnav she knew; or thought she did.

"There are times," Arnav whispered as he reached for Parul's hand and caressed it gently before holding it, "when you are left with no other options. It becomes necessary..."

"For what?" Parul mumbled.

Arnav moved closer as he covered the space that was separating them. They were so close that they were able to feel the warmth of each other's breath.

"Closure." Arnav responded, and Parul felt his hand around her waist before it touched the gun she was clutching in her hand. Parul felt her heart in her throat before she felt his lips on hers.

A few heartbeats later, Parul felt a sharp object piercing her body. Before she took in what had happened, blood had started gushing from the bullet wound. Apparently Arnav had a gun and he had shot her with it. Parul felt Arnav leaving her hand before she staggered back and flopped down on the sofa.

"Why?" Parul said pensively.

"When this is all over, I want you to remember me," Arnav mumbled, ignoring her question, "not as a night that I am, but someone who met the beautiful morning that you are."

Parul gathered all her strength as she clutched the gun Jayesh had given her, her hands betraying the feeling she still had for Arnav, and

In Their Shoes

for a moment, she thought she couldn't do it. But then the lopsided frame caught her attention, and fresh tears rolled down her cheeks as she pointed the gun at him and pulled the trigger.

EPILOGUE

The moment Arnav found out that Parul was holding a gun, Jayesh's words started making sense to him. It was Jayesh, Arnav deduced, who had orchestrated everything. Arnav wished there was another way of handling this.

"You are a monster," a disembodied voice hissed near Arnav's ear, 'you don't deserve to live.'

It was time to put an end to this, Arnav realised and pulled out the gun he was carrying. He had never imagined that out of all people, it would be Parul on whom he would need to use it. He positioned the gun so that the bullet wouldn't do any serious damage to her and pulled the trigger. He then stood there and saw Parul stagger back before she fell on the couch. He stood riveted to the spot and waited for her to react.

And then, another shot rang out.

People say that when you are dying, you see your life flashing in front of your eyes, and yet, all Arnav saw, as the blood started gushing out where the bullet had hit him, was Parul. Arnav felt weak in his knees as he felt himself losing control over his body, and the next moment he dropped on the ground, lifeless.

"In Their Shoes – Interesting name."

A female voice pulled Arnav out of his thoughts, and he found himself back in the room, facing Radhika. Arnav looked to his left to find Mithila sitting next to him. Arnav looked back at Radhika, who closed the book and smiled at him.

It took Arnav some time to gather himself.

"One last question before you both leave." Radhika continued.

"Shoot." Arnav said, rubbing the part of his chest where it still hurt.

"How do you write the stories so efficiently, as if they are your stories?"

Arnav looked at Mithila before looking back at Radhika and explained.

"I believe this world is nothing but a gigantic library, and we all are nothing but characters from one book or another, playing our parts, knowingly or unknowingly, willingly or unwillingly."

Radhika listened with rapt attention.

"Have you ever thought about why you don't remember things about your childhood – the days right after you were just born? maybe there is no science to it, and it simply happens because that part of the story is not written from your point of view, but from someone else's – like your parent's, maybe that's why they remember it?"

"Have you ever thought about what déjà vu is," Arnav continued, "the feeling that whatever we are experiencing has happened before? What if there is no science to it as well but a simple explanation; someone is rereading our story, after a long time. I mean that's how I look at the world. Maybe that's how everything is."

When Arnav noticed their puzzled faces, he simply stopped.

"I am sorry, but I don't think I am following you." Radhika looked stumped.

Arnav contemplated for a few seconds before he responded.

"Well, when I write the characters, I put myself in their shoes. I mean, I don't just write the stories. I live them…"